THE PLAYER AND THE PRINCE

AN
EVERLANDS CYCLE
NOVELLA

J.C. RYCROFT

BATTLEWARRIOR
PRESS

A BattleWarrior Press book

First published in Australia in 2025 by BattleWarrior Press

Ebook first published in 2025 by BattleWarrior Press

Visit the author's website at www.JCRycroft.com

Print ISBN: 978-1-923055-04-9 | Ebook ISBN: 978-1-923055-03-2

First edition

Cover by Fay Lane

Illustrations by Myfanwy Cadwallader

Developmental editing by Cameron Montague Taylor of The AuthorShip Publishing and Editorial Services

Copy and line editing by Rachelle Wright of R. A. Wright Editing

Proofreading by Nay Merrill of Nay's Notations

For all the women the world calls broken;

Who are survivors: righteous, incandescent, and clear-eyed.

May you find your way to everything you are owed.

CONTENTS

AUTHOR NOTE

This novel is not all puppies and sunshine, I'm afraid, and there's some naughty language, dark events, and explicit content.

For a full content note (including a comprehensive set of trigger warnings), which I'd encourage you to check if you're wondering "what exactly do they mean by dark, though?" please see the very final page of the book or visit the book's online home: www.jcrycroft.com/the-player-and-the-prince

CHAPTER ONE

Somehow every time I return to Scyless, I find my heart in my throat, but tonight there's even more riding on it. These kinds of nerves are not common for me anymore, but my strategy for dealing with them is still the same as it's always been: I work at my face until I know that it's as perfect as I can get it. It means I have one less thing - worrying about how I look - to have running through my head while I'm trying to perform, whether on or off the stage.

The Duchess has never skimped on our change rooms, but the glass she's provided this time is brand new, and it makes applying my cosmetics so much simpler. I'm glad of it. I buff out the kohl with a small dense sponge, giving my green eyes a smoky frame.

Usually these days it takes significant power in the audience to raise my anxiety. A Duke, maybe, or at least a Marquess. Killeen is always extremely tense when we perform before men of that status, and it makes him irritable and unkind. But while Elouise is a Duchess, it's not her power, or what it might mean for me that makes me nervous. Not quite.

"You always put more effort in for her," Pearlene says. "Scyless is a backwater and she's practically forgotten at court." She puts down a stool next to me and plunks down on it, meeting my gaze in the mirror. "What am I missing?"

"She likes girls," Delina says bluntly, and I watch my own eyes narrow. She chortles, loud and delighted at getting a reaction out of me.

I sigh noisily, pouting at myself in the glass and don't answer. "She… she is pretty remarkable," Melia puts in, hesitant, her eyes darting to my reflection. She is always so cautious around me. I wonder for the umpteenth time whether Killeen has asked her to try and keep me on side. He knows if I leave it'll impact his bottom line, though that's not why I stay - at least I think it's not. I give her a small, encouraging smile, and she goes on. "She's the King's cousin and sat on his advisory council. She was a force at court before she left."

"Oh yes, I'm sure that's why Liv's doing her face like the King himself is in the audience," Delina replies sarcastically. "Nothing to do with the fairly impressive collection of dildos she's reputed to have." She hoots with laughter and the others join in, Melia's eyes flitting to my reflection as she makes a scandalized noise.

"I won't pretend the dildos don't play a role," I say, sweeping around to face the room, angling my chin like the fanciest jade from Pastira. "She's better hung than most men I've fucked. And you know I know from cock."

They laugh, the delicious, full-throated laughter of women talking of sex together, and I wait until they stop, a wicked smile on my face. "But if all the world sees the Duchess when she's ice, well, this face means I get to see her when she's …" I draw out the pause dramatically, and smile internally as they all lean slightly towards me in anticipation. I guess the cosmetics are doing their job. "Fire." I say in a stage whisper. "So I think it's worth the effort," I finish in my normal voice, eyebrow raised.

The little crowd of players grins and whoops, and next they're telling their own stories: about Pearlene's preferred fuck in Scyless and how he'd left her barely able to walk last time. And Melia talks longingly about the tongue attached to a Pastiran cloth merchant, and Delina about a woman with thighs to die for, and the conversation shifts its focus from me and my face.

I turn back a critical eye to the glass, dabbing more carmine across the full round of my bottom lip and into the points of my Cupid's bow. Tugging free a fine dark curl on each side to frame my face, I double-check the rest of my hair will stay in its pins until the right moment.

It's not entirely my face that earns me a place in Elouise's bed, I don't think. She's not like men; it's more than just the pretty and performance. But something about her makes me want to look my best. I can never quite work out what it is about her that makes me react like this.

Is it just the sex? I wonder for the fiftieth time. Last time, Elouise had tied me to one of the posts on her enormous four-poster bed, and played me like a gods-bedamned fiddle - almost beyond even my extensive capacity for dissembling. I narrow my gaze at myself in the mirror. Maybe that's it. Amongst the hundreds I've slept with, a bare handful have seen an honest reaction from me.

Just the memory of her body pressed to mine makes my breath get short, the pupils in my green eyes dilating. She likes to take inspiration from the plays we perform and that one had had my character strapped to the mast by pirates. The character's end had been death; under Elouise's direction, my end had been the little rendition, reached after an age spent dancing on the rather delightful precipice. I swear I lost consciousness that time.

The Duchess can fuck.

My lips curve and I nod at my reflection, pulling down the chemise I'm wearing to tint my areolas as well. But I know it's not really that she's found her way close to honesty from me. This time, the usual excitement is overlaid by the knowledge that I'm not just enjoying her company this time around. This time around I need something from her. She is the solution to my problem, I think, but that means I have to find a way to ask for something, or manipulate it from her. And she's nobody's fool. Baldly asking for what I need feels vulnerable but she's too smart to easily play.

I've managed to talk Killeen into having us perform "The Lady's Choice," thankfully without having to agree to sleep with him, as he keeps badgering me to. It's getting exhausting, seeking ways to turn him down while preserving his ego. Killeen's is probably the best troupe there is in Rescalin, but he's grouchier than Picton was, more short-sighted and anxious around powerful people... and it's getting dicier, keeping his violence from me. No way he'd let me keep a lover on, like Picton had. I'd had freedom then, but I have more money now. And there is no denying that coin gives me options.

But I need a solution - something to make Killeen grateful to me without having to fuck him. And enabling us to join the annual competition to select the Royal Theatrical Troupe would have to be a gift he'd recognize, surely? It's also something that he can't do himself: his patron is a mere Baron, too low in standing to write the letter of recommendation to the King that would let us enter. But a Duchess...

I blow on my breasts to dry the color, my nipples crinkling into wakefulness, and swear at Killeen in my head again. I don't like being forced to ask for things from Elouise. It muddies waters already made more complex by our difference in status. It's been simple and easy so far, but only because I've not sought anything from her, and she's not sought anything from me. Except sex and companionship, whenever I pass through. No promises, no being beholden. No ties to bind.

Why do men always wind up spoiling things?

If the prospect of having to use my relationship with Elouise to win myself safety from Killeen's hard hands has a line appearing between my brows, anticipation of her reaction to seeing me on stage as Sarine in "The Lady's Choice" nonetheless makes me smile. She starts out the play beautiful but proper, and by the end is disheveled, her hair loose, chemise slipping from her shoulders, and she's singing bawdy songs full-throated in a bar. I am looking forward to seeing how Elouise plans to contribute to Sarine's departure from the rules of her society after the performance.

The door bangs open. "Five minutes to curtain," Stemen bellows into the room. "Positions, now!" The room bursts into activity, women squeezing out the door.

"Melia! Lace me in!" I cry, leaping to my feet and catching up the green costume. The girl doesn't even fumble the laces, just presses her knee against my backside, twists hard, and the dress is pulled firm against every curve, the flare of the skirts generous. I shuffle my breasts in the chemise until the upper swells carve twin curves below my collar bones. "Alright?" I ask, giving her a brilliant smile as I turn towards the door. She nods, mouth falling open like she can't find words, and the star struck blush that floods her cheeks makes me grin. Better confirmation than any compliment.

I scuttle into place in the wings, catching up my fan from Karon, one of the stage hands, who rolls his eyes, grins and mouths 'break a leg!' And then as the skirl of the pipes announces the first scene, I raise my head high and sweep onto the stage.

My gaze immediately finds Elouise, dressed in her favorite pale gray-blue, her silver hair piled up behind a tiara of glittering diamonds, seated on her Duchess's throne in the center of the room. A slow smile blooms across her face at the sight of me, all promise and plans, and I feel my own cheeks pink up in response.

But despite the distraction, I don't miss a single cue all night. Not even when I appear on stage in my transparent chemise and a drunkard in the bar tosses a large cup of ale at me, soaking it through to reveal my carefully tinted breasts.

While the crowd roars with laughter and salacious comment both, Elouise merely leans her chin in her hand, one long slim finger resting still against her lips. What is she thinking? Desire is so intense it's almost painful, spiking through me, but I catch my breath and let my voice soar into the final song.

A tall elderly lady collects me from the dressing room after the performance has finished - I've just been refreshing my makeup and lacing myself back into the green silk of my original costume. She leads me through the quiet castle to Elouise's rooms. In a sumptuous lounge, she says, "Her Grace says to make yourself comfortable. She won't be long." She gestures with an elegant hand at a side table set with fruit and wine and curtsies before closing the door gently behind her.

I pile a small plate high with fruit, then pour myself a glass of wine. Elouise always has the best, and I struggle to eat before a performance. Afterwards I'm always hungry; though tonight my appetite hasn't returned in a rush like it usually does. I still can't work out how I'm going to ask for the letter I need from her. Or how to make sure she can't see the desperation or need behind it.

I settle myself onto a chaise longue, unbuckling my heeled shoes and kicking my feet free. There's something delightful about how easy it is to feel like I've rebelled amongst these aristocratic trappings: the carved wood of the furniture glowing in the light from several cut-glass lanterns. The wine is fine and round on my tongue, complex enough to be sophisticated but still easy to drink. I sip at it and munch on grapes and strawberries.

By the time there's noise at the door, I'm no longer thinking of Killeen or the King. The wine - and time spent pondering that finger tapping against that lip - has made a molten heat of my blood. I rise, and let every last iota of desire show in my gaze. Elouise enters, smiling lightly. Her smile deepens at the sight of me, and my expression, and she turns to someone behind her, muttering softly. They leave, and she crosses the room to me.

"It is lovely to see you once more, Livinia," she murmurs, and the vibration in her low voice makes me shiver.

I curtsy deeply, but don't take my gaze off her. No submissive dipping of the eyes for me. One corner of her mouth curls up. She cups my face gently in her hands and bends to press soft lips against first one cheek and then, skimming her lips lightly across mine - a frightful tease - to the other. Desire traces the path that the wine has already flowed through, and my heartbeat skitters.

She turns away to fill her own wine glass, and I nearly fall to my knees without her hands on me. For the hundredth time I wonder what it is about her that makes me feel like this. I am the one who crooks a little finger at others and has them tumble in piles at my feet. It makes my head spin to watch myself slide so easily into submission with her.

"Did you enjoy the performance?" I ask.

She turns around, red wine in a round, long-stemmed glass. It refracts light into a scatter of rainbows across her face. "I did," she says softly. "I always enjoy seeing you perform. But I have happened across something of a difficulty for tonight's... plans."

"Oh?" The light of her gaze is silver, the color her eyes turn in desire, so I know it cannot be too insurmountable a difficulty.

She gestures at the chaise longue, and we both settle onto it, an agonising arm's length between us. "'The Lady's Choice,'" she says musingly. "So it was called, and yet the only options set before her were men." Her gaze falls to my lips and my breath hitches. "And it seems she chose one of them in the end."

"You wanted Sarine to choose a woman?" I ask, and I'm shocked at how breathless I sound. "Despite... well, how our world works?"

She smiles a little wickedly. "I don't imagine that your troupe would maintain their standing were they to make such an adjustment to the play," she says, then sips her wine. My gaze is glued to where her lips touch the glass. "Though I've seen you play as a man... and perhaps that would have been more interesting. But it made me wonder... if a woman were offered whatever she wanted, is it so inevitable that she would choose a man? And would she choose only one?"

I'm so distracted by desire I can hardly hear her words, but I make an effort to respond meaningfully. "Are you asking if *I* would?" I laugh. "Sarine is positively staid compared to me, I think!"

She chuckles low, and I revel in the sound of it. "Well precisely. Exactly whose dreams of womanhood unleashed are they, then, after all?"

I pause, my mind awakening once more as I follow her reasoning. "What she chooses in the end does look an awful lot like what our world thinks is appropriate for women to choose." I tilt my head. "I mean, she does break a whole bundle of rules, singing in a pub in a chemise... and she has placed desire over duty more than once. Lost the backing of her aristocratic family."

"She does. But she goes home with one man's ring on her finger. The promise of motherhood and monogamy. Is it not astonishing that women's true freedom apparently must end in marriage, one man and the loss of whatever privileges she might have had, all because she owned her desire?"

Her tone is acerbic, and it's almost a comfort as I realize that like Sarine, Killeen is ensuring owning my desires is a complicated dance to keep myself safe.

I find myself sitting very still, thinking about what it's going to do to my desires, here and now, with Elouise, to know that I have to make a request of her to keep Killeen from violence.

She shrugs. "Of course many women will say that marriage *is* their free choice and who could gainsay them? It is not as if we have a second world set just to one side, where we could see what women might choose if the world required something different of them."

"I have heard stories, though," I say slowly, shoving Killeen's presence firmly out of my head. Tomorrow is soon enough for pragmatics. At least one night of reminding the Duchess and myself of what we are to each other without men in the room. "Not of a second world of course." I give a laugh. "But of the Rovers..."

"Ah yes, the Rovers. Did you know that they built this castle?" Elouise gestures her glass at the walls of the room. "Apparently a woman from over east fell in love with a Rover woman. That woman became the elder of her nation, and together they built this."

"Scyless was built by two women, married?" I laugh at the scandalized note in my own voice. "Listen to me: apparently unthinkable even for someone like me, who makes a habit of ignoring all the stupid rules. Was this before or after Rescalin was created?"

"In the midst of her birth pangs, as far as I can tell," Elouise says. "But the truth is likely buried deep. Enough of entertaining history and second worlds. Have you finished your wine?"

I upend the glass into my mouth and smile brilliantly at her, desire like an ember blown back to flame. "I have. And have you decided how you wish to corrupt Sarine?"

Elouise's cool gaze rests on me, thoughtful, and heat skitters over my skin. "I had thought about that," she murmurs, swaying closer to me, shifting on the chaise. She draws the back of her fingertips down the side of my face, and I gulp at the unerring precision in her voice. "When it comes to Sarine, well... as you said, her desires wound up being rather... uninspired."

Her mouth is a bare inch from mine, and I can feel the heat of her body pressed against my front, the scalding spark where the bare skin of the top of my cleavage presses against the fine silk of her dress. She pauses. "You may say no, and play at Sarine if you wish, and I will wear multiple leather cocks and take you however many times you wish. I'm sure I will be quite satisfied with that." She brushes her lips against mine and I nearly fall into her, I so long for that kiss. "But if we're talking about *this* lady's choice, I would far rather explore what your desires, Livinia, unleashed, might look like."

My breath shivers out in a barely suppressed moan as I realize what she is asking of me.

Does she even know what she's asking?

It feels like a risk; being honest always has. I avoid it at all costs, generally. As a player, I've been good enough that one way or another, in my play I usually can get what I need out of the person in front of me. Whatever that is. It's been a place to sleep, or coin, or protection, or a place in a troupe, or a thousand other things. I learned early not to entrust myself to others, and now that habit is bone-deep. Especially when I fuck.

But her eyes are more silver than I've ever seen them, and it feels like a dare, almost. A bare echo of what Des had once managed to draw from me, in her unsettlingly direct way, toying with the line between dominance and otherwise, between true feeling and playfulness. A split-second ache trembles in my heart, but Des is long gone - she chose that - and it's habit now to deny the hurt. It's not like it was the worst betrayal I've survived.

And Elouise is here and she's beautiful and smart and she's turned on by asking for my honesty. Her gaze is unrelenting, but I know that I can say no, and we would still have a night of pleasure. So this is a decision of what I want.

And so I inhale a breath, almost a gasp, and kiss her intently, my hands gripping the slender length of her against me, and my tongue teasing into her mouth. When I feel the moan suppressed in the back of her throat hum into my flesh, I pull away and smile, arch and satisfied. "If you are sure, Elouise, that you want to see what I want unleashed, well, far be it from me to deny you."

She laughs briefly, the sound a chime. "Well let's see what your unleashed desires might have to say about denial first shall we?"

I have never known such pleasure and I have *known* pleasure.

I plead.

I never plead. Ever. Only ever with Des, before, and only ever in play.

My body has given up a crashing wave of pleasure a good half dozen times already, and all I am longing for is more. I whimper, the sound of helplessness and want and a body no longer able to seek out its desires. I can only hope that she will be able to fulfill them. That she will want to.

"More?" she asks softly.

"More," I manage to say. "Gods, please, *please*, Elouise, more."

Elouise twists her wrist where three of her fingers are buried inside my cunt, and I gape at the sense of fullness as she adds another, adding an extra slick of oil, her thumb tucked in tight. I press my heels into the bed, the edge of fear making me want to pull away. She gazes up at me, and I glance down to see her smile. "You're doing so well," she murmurs before she presses her mouth tight against my clit once more.

Tears prick in my eyes. I refuse to think about why; refuse thought altogether. Sensation skates over my skin, tingling into pleasure and I relax once more. Her fingers reach deeper inside me, curling upwards, and I gape again. I've never felt so full and all I want is more.

"Has anyone ever done this to you?" she asks softly, and I watch as she firmly presses one long-fingered hand against the soft round of my belly, aligned with where her fingers curl inside me.

And I gasp, mouth wide, as a deep pleasure, darker somehow than the light sparkling bliss of her mouth working my clit, catches deep within me. I groan, the sound guttural and unguarded, and my body arches around her hand. She smiles, and the delight on her face warms me. And then her lips are once more wrapped around my clit, her hand inside me reaching deeper...

I gape, soundless, unable to draw breath, teetering, teetering...

And then I gasp and cry, long and ragged, as the orgasm catches hold of me, tosses me upward into the stars, and lets me fall apart into blissful oblivion, anchored by the thudding heartbeat in my cunt.

CHAPTER TWO

I wake to sunshine angling into the room through a crack between the curtains. I stretch, the ache in my cunt making me groan, a sound so lascivious it makes me chuckle aloud. It's delicious. I don't remember ever being so thoroughly fucked.

Maybe there's something to this whole honesty thing.

Maybe.

I roll over and stare at the motes of dust dancing in the ray of light, relieved to find Elouise's side of the bed is empty.

I'd let her see me. Untucked myself for her.

I wait for the dread to unfurl deep within me.

When it comes, it's like rage; fierce, unrelenting and awful.

I focus on calming my breathing, and watch the motes as if my life depends on it.

Maybe it does.

The dread is an echo of grief. I know it, but it doesn't undo it. It's as familiar as the constellation of freckles on the back of my own hand.

I'd been on the street since my mother had died when I was four, and Isharin had been, I'd thought, my new family. He'd taken me in when I was seven, given me clothes and food and somewhere warm and safe to sleep. He'd smiled at me, taught me to read and write, how to pick pockets and beg for money well on the streets. He'd told me I was special. Pretty. I'd been too smart to believe him at first, but after four years of unrelenting kindness, I loved him.

So when he sold me to a flesh trader, barely eleven and still flat-chested, it had been the most profound heartbreak I'd ever known, worse even than what I remembered of my mother dying.

It was the first betrayal, but it was far, so far, from the last.

I had promised myself I would never let myself be devastated like I had been over Isharin. No trust, no exposure, no love meant no chance of heartbreak.

But there had been more. Most without my love, and it made it easier to recover from.

Every betrayal after that first one was like an echo, a reminder that I hadn't concealed myself well enough. Every time I promised myself again that that was the last time.

And with each new hurt, I'd learned to tuck myself further away, deep within. To only ever play for what I wanted, and to never let anyone catch a glimpse of what I might truly want or why. To find a way to get what I needed without anyone ever seeing what that might be.

There's a quiet click as the door opens. Elouise enters, carrying a tray, and I would smile at the Duchess playing at maid for me if the terror were not so very intense.

"Good morning," she murmurs, turning to set the tray on a side table.

I press down the dread, force myself to play. "Good morning," I say brightly.

"Oh." She gives me a grave look. "I see."

Panic redoubles in my gut and I shove it down. She mustn't see me. See this.

Playing. Playing for safety. "Is that breakfast?" I leap to my feet, ignoring the ache between my thighs. I dance up to her and give her a long, chaste kiss on the cheek, then a broad grin. "I hope I didn't keep you from eating. Have you been up long?"

"Not so long," she says quietly. "Livinia, I promise you, you have nothing to fear here."

I laugh, and hope that only I can hear the false note of it. "Fear? We are inside a well-guarded castle that can only be entered via a causeway and even then only when the tide wills it." I grin at her, plucking a grape from the tray and popping it into my mouth. "Safe as houses, surely?"

She gives me look that manages somehow to be open and accepting and also amused by my play. It doesn't matter; I still have to play, even knowing she sees through it. There's submission and then there's utter exposure. We play at the edge of that precipice often enough, but I know myself well enough to know that if I lose my footing, a plunge over that cliff would destroy me. I'd disappear into Elouise in a heartbeat and I cannot give myself over like that. "Well yes, we are unlikely to be the target of attack, that is true."

"And Killeen knows that the longer he lets me spend with you, the more likely we'll be invited back next time. So! Shall we eat?" The panic has eased, with the evidence that she's not likely to push me for honesty again now, but the dread is a hollow gaping pit. Hunger might be part of that, so best to reduce what I can.

"Let's eat," she agrees. "But shall we sit on the balcony? I have a robe for you."

And she does - embroidered silk in a green that matches my eyes. I wrap it around me and tug free my black curls, which are matted and clumped with old sweat. "I'm going to need a bath before I find the troupe," I mutter to myself.

"And about a gallon of water to drink, I suspect." She gives me a wicked little smile. "You were... rather damp."

"You did work me hard," I agree comfortably. With every moment she lets my performance stand, the dread ebbs back a little.

"I worked *you* hard?" She chuckles quietly. "I've never known anyone's desire for pleasure to press beyond my physical capacity to fulfill them, but you, my dear, came close!"

This is safer, this gentle banter. I smile at her, and eat as she asks me questions about our tour, about the places I've seen. She enjoys me describing the world to her. Sometimes I wonder if she misses being out in it. I still am not sure why she locks herself away here.

"So, my dear," she says softly. "Tell me about your plans."

"My plans?" I grin at her and shrug, but inside I sharpen my attention. This is the moment to find a way to get that letter for Killeen. But first a reminder of our connection... "I plan to find my way into your bed at least one more time this morning before I head back to Killeen. Back to... oh but you have no need to listen to all of that."

"I am always interested in your life, Livinia."

I sigh, puffing out my cheeks. Here we go. "I'm not sure how much longer I'll be able to stay with the troupe. Killeen keeps pressuring me into his bed. I slept with him before I joined the troupe," I explain. "But sleeping with the troupe leader seems like a bad plan. It always has. And I don't want him."

"Will you join another troupe then? Go back to Picton's? And that girl you carried off from her village, what was her name?"

The thought of Des makes the confused burble of dread rise within me again. "Dinah," I murmur, giving the same false name I'd always given Elouise for Des. I couldn't even have said why I lied, exactly, except that somehow the memory of Des felt too precious to have it pinned out like a butterfly in a case, for her gaze. "But no. I had one thought."

She gives me a shrewd look, but leaves space for me to speak. I give her a quick glance, dipping eyes from hers before she can see how conscious I am of the risk my next words pose to the careful balance of our relationship. "We're a good troupe, Killeen's, probably good enough to spend a season or two as the Royal Theatrical Troupe, really. But Killeen is too afraid of power to build our reputation properly. It makes him grasping and servile and resentful." I smile half-heartedly, not quite meeting her eyes. "Our patron remains a Baron, while comparable troupes are winning the support of Dukes and even the King." It's hard to make my mouth say the words. They feel blunt, like a hammer. "But I wondered if you might write to the King a letter of introduction in support of our participation in the Royal Theatrical Troupe competition this year?"

She gazes at me evenly, and I know she can feel the shift my request is making in what lies between us. "If it will help, Livinia, of course. I'm unclear how this will be of assistance, but it is no hardship to recommend Killeen's troupe to the King. You are all skilled players."

"I hope that it's sufficient replacement for, well," I gesture at my body. "For me."

She twitches an eyebrow, and I look away so I'm not so acutely conscious of her every expression. "And if it isn't?"

"I'd likely have to move on. The problem is that Killeen is probably the best and everyone knows it." I make a face. "I'm not sure how to manage it so that it doesn't appear that I'm the problem. Like *I'm* the problem, when it's really that he just will not stop propositioning me." I give a sardonic, irritated smile. "Listen to me go on. These aren't your problems to solve, Elouise. I will manage them. The letter would help, though. Pastira will bring more options; so will court, I think."

"Perhaps it's time to think longer term then?"

I give her a quizzical look. "Longer term?"

"Surely this is the moment for it? You are at the top of your game. Recognized across the nation. You have money. But you won't always have these things. What do you want to do with them?" She pauses, tracing a fingertip against the rim of her glass. "What do you want to do with your future?"

I shift uncomfortably, rubbing my shoulders against the silk of the robe. I shifted our relationship. Is this the moment she tries to claim me, finally, after all this time? I would evaporate in that. "Oh... I don't think of futures. Today is enough."

Her eyes on me are mild as she says, "Is it?"

I swallow, schooling my features so as not betray anything. "It is."

She presses her lips together and even the gentle reproof is scalding. I suppress my reaction. "I worry for you, that is all, Livinia. I want you to have a future you will continue to enjoy. And I've seen so many smart, beautiful women hit their stride, find the apex of their career, and then before they know it, they are on the downwards turn, losing power and money and being forced to find their way however they can." She sips from her glass. "I know that playing at being a jade can be profitable in the right circumstances. And that right now, you are making enough money that you can choose when the circumstances are right.

Because it is a play. But in the wrong ones, when you have no other options, it can leave you unprotected against all kinds of misuse."

"I'm aware," I say in a low voice, trying not to betray the extraordinary combination of emotions roiling through me. I've fought hard to grasp back agency from those who would have kept it out of reach forever. Constant vigilance - is that what she's telling me my freedom will cost? Does she know where she sits in that landscape?

She puts her chin on her hand, gazing at me. "But that is all about the risk, and that's a poor way to make a decision. What would you *like* to do?"

"Do?... That feels like a big question. Now if you ask me what I'd like... I know what I'd like. To no longer be at the whim of any troupe leader. Or really any man," I say, self-mocking. "Perhaps we could find that second world we talked about, and all the women could go there and all the men could stay here." I press a finger against my lips musingly. "Yes... and perhaps there could be some kind of special border..." I trail off. Her eyes are alight. "What is it? You look like either I've said something brilliant or you have come up with something to match?"

"No, but - truly, Livinia. What do you wish for?"

I bite my lip a moment, wondering. How many times have I rolled my eyes over the cliche and familiar melodrama of our fare? How many times have I pondered what other stories we could be telling: Sarine choosing otherwise; a world in which the impossible is made possible. Sometimes I think the strict limitations on the stories we can tell is where power really lies in this world; what other stories could I make possible. My arms prickle into gooseflesh. "I... I know it's not possible; they'd never let me. But I do think sometimes about, well, about how many Sarines there are in the stories we tell on our stages. And how many other stories there are to tell..." I swallow, not meeting her eyes.

"Would you... lead your own troupe?" She asks slowly, putting it together. "You'd be the first woman, if my history is right. And you could do it in your sleep. Well, you might need some assistance to begin with, but it's really just about paying for the right expertise." She sits back in her chair, smiling. "You'd give any of these men a run for their money. It would be quite something to see."

My reaction as she begins this little speech is to try to find a way to say no, but this last thought makes the hair rise on the back of my neck. Challenging Killeen for the top spot? It sounds... impossible. And incredible.

"You think I could?" I say softly, wonderingly, not really letting myself believe it. "Really?" As soon as the word is out, the enchantment in it clear, the dread spirals up again inside me. Exposure. Have I given myself away?

She gazes at me, those cool gray eyes contemplative. "I think you could." She makes a moue of her mouth. "But you would need the King's sign off to give you a way in with the aristocracy. I would be able to be your first patron then, and you can skip the years of building an audience. I can write you an introduction, since you'll be at court anyway, for the competition."

She's given me everything I've asked for, and I cannot have her ask me about the possibility she's put in front of me. A possibility that I can't even let be real yet.

I rise and cross to stand above her. She raises her gaze to meet mine, yet despite the fact that she's seated and I'm standing, somehow there's still no doubt. She's in control. "I am very grateful, my lady," I murmur, letting my voice vibrate. "You must let me make it up to you."

And as I speak I lean over her, loosening the tie on her robe, flipping it open to reveal the pink of her nipple, puckering up fast in the cool breeze. I run a gentle finger down the fine golden-pale skin from her collarbone, circling it, then rubbing the pad of my thumb across the pebbled surface. She catches her breath and I glance up to meet her eyes, the pupils rapidly expanding despite the sunlight.

I sink to my knees on the stone balcony, tugging at the tie. Somehow it feels right to be kneeling before her. "May I?" I ask softly, and my breath is coming short at the thought of burying my mouth in her cunt.

Her eyes are dancing. "I do not doubt we will shock some gardeners, but I will try to be quiet."

I smile, spreading the robe wide, breathless at the sight of the dark triangle of tightly curled hair. "You may try," I agree, letting the lightness carry me. "But I will not collude with you in this horror of repression; you should know that." I slide my hands down the pale golden skin of her thighs, to her knees, and gently spread them. "It is against my beliefs."

The scent of her rises into the air and my eyes shutter closed at the promise of it. Her cunt lies before me, glistening dark pink in the morning light, and it's all I can do to play it out, to draw up her arousal. I breathe out, letting the tickle of it trail over her skin. Her cunt twitches and I know she felt it.

"No one has ever called me repressed before," she tells me, a laugh behind her words. "You should know that."

"But then, has anyone made you come on a balcony before?" I murmur, shifting closer, my lips brushing against the soft fuzz.

"Not yet."

And then I press my mouth to her heavenly cunt and lose myself in the sound of her gasp.

CHAPTER THREE

The troupe are bunked down in a large disused barracks, and by the time I find them, the sun is drifting past its zenith and they're drinking.

"If it's not our favorite little jade," Killeen says in greeting, his voice already fuzzy round the edges and sharp with aggression. He's draped into a chair, and his large stein drips beer into a puddle on the stone.

"Earning everyone's keep, as usual," I say, too sweet, and roll my eyes at him when he glares. "Well, if you don't want to be insulted, don't insult me! There's really no need to be such a grouch, Killeen. It's deeply unattractive." I hurry on before he can clamber out of his chair and bellow at me. "Anyway, I've done you a favor. If we play the next few days well, the Duchess will write a letter to the King, recommending us for this year's competition for Royal Theatrical Troupe."

"She will? Liv, I - Excellent! This is excellent!" Killeen is astonished and delighted now, leaping out of his chair. The rest of the troupe come alive with chatter, and it makes me smile. Killeen catches Melia up out of her chair, swinging her around in an impromptu jig. She smiles and laughs up at him, her creamy pale skin pinking up over her cheeks; and I wonder that he, the leader of a troupe of players, can't spot the play. Or maybe he does, and just doesn't care.

He sends her spinning and breathless back to her spot in the circle, then turns to me, and his hand is hard on my hip. The other is wrapped so tight around my fingers that the bones creak. Ugh. I give in and graciously dance a couple of steps, then spin myself into a turn that lets me spiral out of his reach. Delina laughs, harsh and unkind, and I send her a sharp look. Last thing we need is someone else pricking at Killeen's pride.

I scoop up a stein of beer, and raise it to him, almost like a shield, before he can turn his fury on me. Despite his stormy scowl, he reluctantly grabs his half-drunk beer and returns the gesture. "She wants us here another few nights," I say, leaning my hip against Stemen's tall-backed chair. "And she hasn't said yes yet, but she's considering it."

"This is going to win us the badge of the Royal Theatrical Troupe!" Killeen's nose turns almost purple in his delight. "If you lot can keep it in your pants, that is! I hear the Queen disapproves of jades at court, as she puts it. Clinging to the old ways, that one, while the rest of the court makes her a hypocrite." He guffaws hugely, his mustache twitching.

"Does this mean we have to plan another few acts? If we're staying longer?" Stemen's gaze is clear. He rarely partakes in beer - says it risks the slow destruction of his career. He means his physique would suffer. Players are so often thought of as vain, but there's little doubt that a pretty face or a brawny chest will compensate for a lack of skill. And Stemen has been in the business for long enough to know.

"Seems that way," Joseph murmurs. He's always low of voice, and occasionally his gaze is so incisive that that dread uncoils in my gut. He's even-tempered and calm, though, which is a relief amongst the prickles of the rest of the troupe. "Liv, did you get a sense of what she'd like to see?"

"More of Liv, I'd warrant!" Delina bellows with laughter as I roll my eyes again.

"Don't think I know that piece," Stemen says quellingly, which only makes Delina laugh harder.

"Perhaps 'The Player and the Prince'?" I suggest. "Or 'The Fall of Sijou'? Either of those would be good performances for the Duchess to mention to the King."

"Always strategizing aren't you?" Killeen sneers.

The disdain stings. I raise my chin, glaring at him. Fuck. Two seconds after I've given him the gift that is meant to keep me safe for months at least, and he's already clawing at me. "Do what you like, Killeen. It's only your fucking troupe."

"Too good to fuck your own troupe, is that what it is?" Killen's face is ugly with jealousy and possessiveness, and he's clearly drunk enough that he doesn't even seem to care that he's changing the subject out of nowhere.

And he wonders why I don't choose him.

"Are you fucking kidding me?!" I plant my hands on my hips, feeling Stemen's solid presence rise just behind me. Thank the gods I know he's on my side. "The woman I chose to fuck last night is probably giving us an entree to the King and now you're angry I didn't choose your..." I search for the word, "Bed?" Delina yowls and laughs as I sneer at him, unable to keep the words back. Even imagining an exit from his control is enough. "Grow up, Killeen. You've built a troupe and a strategy good enough to get us before the King. This is not the moment to be throwing it all away because I don't want to fuck you."

"Plus she's not that good a fuck," Delina puts in cattily.

"It doesn't matter whether she is or not," Joseph says, and I turn to meet his even gray gaze. "Because whatever else is the case, she gets to choose who she takes to her bed. End of." His voice is mild, and his long slender limbs, hooked up over the arms of his chair, seem entirely relaxed; but his gaze is fixed on Killeen. "And besides, she's right that 'The Fall of Sijou,' would work well for the audience. Plus it gives Stemen the chance to flex some of that impressive muscle on stage, and you know how the aristocrats love that."

Stemen blushes, as he always does when Joseph compliments him. "I think either of Liv's suggestions would work," he adds.

Melia, back in her seat, leans forward. "I like the second act in 'The Player and the Prince' better, but the climax in 'Sijou' really can't be matched. And endings matter more than middles, especially for this kind of thing - leave them impressed."

I smile, sliding backward into a spare seat and take a big gulp of my beer. "I mean maybe there's another option? But we want something that we've practiced enough but not performed so much it'll be stale."

And with that, the room bursts into chatter. Killeen is back in his seat, drinking deep out of his cup. I can feel his eyes on me as everyone talks, but I ignore him entirely.

As I watch the others discussing the journey to Pastira and the best way to earn the King's favor, I can't help but ponder Elouise's proposal. Could I really lead a troupe? Would poaching my fellow players be worth Killeen's fury? Would it even be possible for him to be more angry than he is now? Who would I prioritize? Perhaps Stemen? We make a good pair on stage, and he's stunning, if you like them heavily muscled. Which many do, both men and women.

"Coin for your thoughts?" Pearlene settles into the chair beside me, a slender pipe between her lips. She's older than most of the rest of us, tending to play mothers and grandmothers in our plays. And witches or crones. "You were all full of ideas a minute ago, and now you're mum."

I give her a rueful smile, and reply in a low voice. "Just tired. I thought he'd be excited about Pastira. I wasn't looking for a fight."

Pearlene shakes her head, drawing hard on her pipe. "You've managed him well, but there's nothing like a woman a man can't get. He's too focused on getting you in his bed now." She gives me a conspiratorial smile, sending blue smoke furling into the air. "It wasn't worth the fuss for me. I just did it, just the once. And made sure I was the least enthusiastic fuck he'd ever had." She grins at me. "I was younger then, pretty still - breasts like melons and legs that ran all the way up to my neck, like they say - but even so, he let me be after that."

An acrid taste fills my mouth. "I'm not going to sleep with him. Not again." The words come out harder than I mean them too and dread coils low in my gut. Can she hear the fragility in them?

She shakes her head again. "And you shouldn't. It wouldn't work anyway. He's angry now; angry and obsessed. Even if you played at being a log, like I did, it wouldn't be enough. He'd be angry you weren't enthusiastic." She makes a smoke ring, then another, larger, to chase it in the air. "He's never going to be satisfied." Her forehead furrows. "I cannot see a resolution, really."

I sigh. Why couldn't he have let the letter from Elouise to the King be enough? "There will be something I can do, I'm sure."

She gives me a sidelong look, measuring. "Mayhap. If there's any a one to find the way, it'll be you. But honest to blessed heaven, Liv. That desire and that fury... and the sense that he's entitled... just be careful, lass."

I take a sip of my beer to cover my thoughts. If Pearlene is warning me off, maybe I really do have to leave. It's true that he's been more persistent than I've seen in most men - usually constant rejection is enough.

I finally glance towards Killeen. Thankfully he's watching the rest of the troupe arguing over our set list. But a moment later, he meets my eyes. He's chewing his mustache and his gaze is stony. "I'll figure it out," I say, sounding more certain than I am. This is my skill after all, and it's kept me pretty safe - making people believe whatever I want them to believe while I get what I want.

"If anyone can, it's you," she says, and I can hear the unease in her voice, as well as the brusque faith in me.

"I'm weary. Didn't get much sleep last night. I'll be back on deck before the performance tonight, don't worry."

"I'll let him know if he asks," she says easily, blowing a long narrow coil slowly into the air.

"Thanks." I set my stein on the table - someone will no doubt get thirsty enough to drink my leavings - and walk away down the hall towards my room.

I wish I didn't feel Killeen's eyes on my back as I do.

CHAPTER FOUR

I settle onto a low stool beside Elouise's armchair and press my head against the warmth of her slender, silk-clad thigh with a sigh. "Something definitely needs to change," I say in a low voice. "It's going to get dangerous, I think."

"With Killeen?" Elouise's voice is sharp. "Is it better if you just stay with me?"

I smile against her, even though a thread of anxiety draws through my gut. I would disappear if I stayed, I'm sure of it. "Are you trying to prove something to those gardeners?" I ask, gently teasing instead. "But no. I don't... I can't just hide here with you."

"Of course not, but... you would be welcome to stay. If the risk is that severe."

I sigh again. "No, I can manage it. But... it's tiring." The dread unfurls in my gut. I don't usually share these kinds of things with anyone - it's a risk, after all. If I entrusted such to anyone - even Pearlene - it would only take a slight twist of the screw for Killeen to pitch her own well being against disclosing my secrets. And so. No one needs to know.

"I understand," she says softly, the tender weight of her hand settling into my curls. "But if the choice is ever between coming here and being harmed, Livinia... there should be no choice about it."

My heart squeezes up into my throat, and I murmur in my own head, no, Liv, you cannot afford love. Not like this. If I sink too deeply into the comfort of this support, I would lose myself forever, I'm sure of it. Lose myself in her. And there's some small voice deep in my soul that adds, She would think she'd won, and even though I know it's unworthy of Elouise, and even though I have cheerfully placed myself in her hands - sometimes literally! - the idea that she could even think she had put one over on me makes me recoil.

I draw myself together. "We leave tomorrow," I say instead of any of that. "And Elouise... if you would earn me my safety between here and the capital, the entree to the King is..." I trail off, half hating that I have to ask even this of her. It stings, like a mayfly on my arse, and I'm twitchy with it.

She is silent for a long moment, and it's all I can do to keep myself from turning my head into her hand. "An entree for Killeen, as we agreed," she murmurs. "And one for the young up-and-coming troupe leader, Livinia Equitor, yes?"

"Yes," I say, reining in the trembling gratitude in my voice. The dread is roiling in my guts now. "Thank you."

"I will also write and see if I can find the names of those in Pastira who hold the expertise you will require to start the troupe itself," she adds quietly. "And I will send it on ahead to Pastira, so it's ready when you arrive. You should meet with them before you make any announcements." She hesitates, and this time I do look up at her. "Livinia... I do not wish to sound discouraging, but it is important to consider the risks that the capital might pose to you."

I smile up at her, a genuine broad grin. "You know that's where I grew up, right? On the streets of Pastira?"

She returns the smile, but there's concern in the line of her brows. "It is not the streets of Pastira that I am thinking of," she replies tartly. "I am sure you have more than enough... wherewithal... to navigate them. It is the court." She pauses, then rises to pour us each a tall glass of a pale sparkling wine. "It's a complicated space, for a woman. And for a woman of your background particularly..."

I draw myself up off the stool, following her across the room. Crossing into her space, I press a kiss into her cheek and then sigh as I dip my head, taking the glass from her hand. The scent of her perfume fills my nostrils, and I can see the slender hairs rise along her neck as I exhale against the skin. Her lips part, and I want to kiss them. The desire gathers in my cunt, and I smile, my eyes dipped from hers.

"I know you know how to play these games of desire," she murmurs softly, a gentle finger turning my head so that she can plant a slow kiss on my lips. "But..." She hesitates. "It is wrong, what happens at court. It is part of why I left. But it is a reality, and I must know that you know. So that you can make the choices that you need to make."

I sigh, letting myself fall back onto a chaise longue, not spilling a drop of my wine by long practice. For a moment, I let my gaze roam across her body. The hard-drawn line of her collarbones; the gentle swell of her breasts, and the gracious line that curves through waist to hips and buttocks. Those slender gray eyes, the subtle pink of her cheeks. She is remarkably beautiful, and all it makes me want to do is please her. And make her gasp. But she seems focused on something specific so I give her a long-suffering smile. "Very well, your Grace. What is it that you need to me to know?"

She swallows, and I wonder what it could be - she seems upset that she has to say it aloud. "If they - the court, I mean - if they see you as a... as one whose work includes sex," she scowls heavily, staring at the wine in her glass, her mouth turned at the corners as if she tastes something bitter. "They will not see you as anything more."

The play of my own desire wisps into nothingness. Wrath comes in the aftermath, a scalding fury that burns in my veins. She would deny me my own way, a voice screams in my head and I hold my body still, my jaw set, making space around it that the resonance of that anger doesn't slide from my mouth. Cautiously, deliberately, focusing on the action, I sip at my wine, waiting for the rage to subside. Did I bring this on, shifting the terms of our relationship by asking for something? She can control nothing, I whisper inside, back to the voice that yet bellows. And slowly, it sinks back into quietude.

"Elouise," I say, aiming for sensible, though it comes out a little terse. "Is this you asking for something specific from me? Because I thought we were clear about what this could be, to each of us. If that has changed..."

Elouise's eyes drift closed as if in pain, and she shakes her head. "No! Blessed heavens, Livinia!" She sounds scandalized, and more animated than I've seen her. "This is not some misguided attempt to manipulate you into monogamy!" She paces, her gaze fixed before her, away from me. "Gods no," she says again. "You and I... our understanding is clear. You offer what you will, and I will do the same. When we can." She shakes her head. "No, it's just... the court can be a den of red-bellied blacks, and I could never forgive myself if I let you go in there without warning!"

A slow breath, and her shoulders settle. "It is not fair, or just. But if you want the King to recognize you as a troupe leader of your own troupe, well... you need to make sure that they can see you as something other than... a jade." She says the word distastefully, and when she glimpses my raised brows, she shakes her head again. "It is ridiculous and unfair, the judgments that they make of those who make their way in the world by having sex. But the judgments do exist. And so, my dear, I cannot let you walk in there not knowing that."

She settles on the chaise longue, a slender hand cupping my bared calf. The contact makes my skin sing. "You are beautiful, and you know it. You know the power of it, and you should use it! And I know you enjoy sex - as you should. My only caution is to understand that especially the men will see you as nothing more than an object if you sleep with them - with any of them. And that if you sleep with one, they will all know. And it may risk your plans."

I give her a weary smile. "The hypocrisy of men, I suppose," I murmur, sipping at my wine again. "This is good, by the way."

"I can barely taste it," she says, the honesty making her voice hard. "Speaking of men's..." She wrinkles her nose, shaking her head as if to free the thoughts. "It frustrates me. And I don't want you to think I agree with them. Or that I'm trying to tie you down." She smiles, a genuine smile this time, and tilts her head. "I love your wild spirit, my dear. I have no desire to tame it, or you." She sighs. "It has been a time since I have been at court. I wearied of it. Of the constant manipulations and jockeying for position. And the hypocrisy of it." She shakes her head again. "Enough." Her hand slides up past my knee, then slowly down my thigh. "It is enough, yes? You understand?"

I meet her gaze, which is turning silver as her fingers push my skirts aside. "I understand," I murmur, and the desire is back, flaring to life like embers exposed to the air. My breath comes short and I watch her for a moment. The suspicious voice in my head is quiet. If it believes her, she's probably telling the truth - and I don't want to leave her wondering. I smile, and reach out to cup her face, drawing her up toward me. "But I'd rather fuck your brains out now, if you don't mind. Your Grace."

This makes her laugh, a low, surprised chuckle that fixes somewhere in the middle of my gut, and I capture her lips with mine. The kiss is intense, leaves me gasping, and she's lying pressed tight against me. I draw up a knee between her legs, grip at her hips. I gaze into her eyes as I run my hand up through the sweet nip of her waist, and then to the heady curve of her breast.

"I should write you your letters," she says softly, a little regretful. "Before we get to the... enjoyable part of the evening."

I pout, playing at disappointed. "Well, if you must," I say grudgingly.

She rises, somehow graceful still, and makes her way across the room to a low desk by a window. "It will take but a moment."

I let the silence grow round, then get up and cross to stare out at the sea beyond the open window. White caps top the waves, and the light of the moon shimmers across the broken surface of the water. Everything is too serious, and I'm feeling a little guilty for the fury I'd felt. Had she known? She can see a lot of me, but surely I'm not fully transparent, even to her? "You know," I murmur softly, trailing fingers along the mantle above the hearth. "I often think that men don't know what they're doing with those cocks of theirs. They're wasted on them."

Another surprised laugh, and she looks up at me. "Are you seeking to distract me from my work here?" Her voice is playfully severe.

"Not at all, your Grace. I'd never do such a thing," I reply soberly, sounding terribly sincere. She snorts in a most unladylike fashion, and it makes me smile. "I see. So you're just trying to tell me that you'd like a leather cock?"

"You do have a rather exceptional collection," I say seriously, grateful that the intensity from earlier has given way finally. "And I thought you might like one..."

Her face lights up with her laughter. "Very well. You go fetch us a couple of cocks. You know where the collection is. And I will finish writing these letters. And then we can spend some time proving to each other that cocks are wasted on men, yes?"

"As you wish, your grace," I say, offering a deep curtsy and holding it until she looks up to see it.

"You are a most lovely distraction, Livinia, and when you bend the knee like that..." Her voice has that resonance in it that makes me shiver, and then she smiles. "Go on, then. And hurry back. I'm nearly done here."

We roll out of Scyless at mid-morning, the Duchess's household turning out to wave us on our way. Elouise herself had breakfasted with me, then pressed two scrolls into my hand. "If it goes awry," she had said, "you can always return here." She'd hesitated then, her fingers cool against my cheek. "Good luck. I look forward to hearing about your adventures."

"You are too kind, Elouise," I murmured, and she'd kissed me thoroughly before she left.

I play that kiss over and over in my mind as two of the guard hold us at the top of the stair that leads down the causeway. Waves crash, drawing back to reveal the stone beneath, forming a slender, silver-bright pathway that disappears as the sea surges in again. "I didn't know the water actually came up over it," Melia says, wide-eyed.

"Is it going to be long before the tide drops enough?" Killeen is grouchy, and his beetling eyebrows make the guards exchange a glance.

"Not long."

"Is it safe to cross while there's still water over it?" Killeen asks.

"The rule in Scyless is never cross when there's even one wave that's reached the road," the red-headed guard says. "Lest you be swept off."

"True of when the tide is on its way out too," his swarthy companion adds. "But it won't be long now. Few minutes, I reckon, but sometimes it has a last few big waves and her Grace wouldn't forgive us if you was to be swept away."

And so I stand with the others, stroking my thumb over my lip, thinking of Elouise's kisses and not even listening to the chatter amongst the troupe.

"A good night then?" Killeen jeers loudly. Definitely directed at me.

I raise my brows. "It was lovely, thank you," I dead-pan, as if I haven't registered the tone of his voice. "And breakfast was delicious too."

"Eating cunt, were we?" Delina squawks.

I raise my eyes to the heavens. "For breakfast? Not this morning. Waffles and berries this morning. Her Grace's chef outdid themselves. How about you?"

"You're like the cat who's got the cream," Pearlene puts in behind me. "What are you celebrating, Delina?"

Delina's gaze slides to Killeen, a look of triumph on her face. Ah. Looks like he's chosen another to warm his bed. I can only hope that it keeps him entertained and away from me. But I glance at Killeen and see there a look of avid, hopeful greed as he stares at me. It looks like Delina was chosen to sting my pride. If it wasn't so awful I'd have to laugh.

I steel myself to find a reply, but fortunately, the guards announce that it's safe for us to be on our way. The sight of my worn little caravan - pulled up under the twisted trees that thrive in the salt air in the courtyard - is both relief and consternation. Somehow spending time in a castle has made it seem particularly small and ragged. I promise myself I'll have it painted in Pastira - surely if the King pays for our performances, we'll have more than enough coin for such things.

I open the door to my little van, climbing inside and dumping my pack onto the bed. It's small and ragged, with all the opulent brocades threadbare. But it's mine. And it promises that no matter what, I can leave and still have somewhere to lay my head.

I remember when I first bought it, back when I was in Picton's troupe. The player I'd bought it off had chosen to take a husband and settle in a small hamlet. Is been all too delighted to take it off her hands. I'd looked right past the worn fabrics and paint - and it felt like security. Independence and security.

I greet Dragon, the horse that pulls it, and he snuffles at my palms. A stolen apple from the Duchesss's breakfast buffet is in my pocket, and when he snorts at it, I give in and offer it to him. He makes a quick inspection of my scent, then crunches it out of my hand. I smile and smooth a hand across the roan's nose. I haul myself up into the driver's seat and urge Dragon forward.

We roll down the long slope that bisects the low stairway up from the causeway, the horses making their uncertainty about the wet known.

"Watch the green patches," the red-headed guard calls. "They're slippery."

I nod and offer a mock salute with the wrong hand, and we make our way, rattling and rumbling across the stone causeway towards the beach.

As we reach the rise of the first dune and find the road that leads away, I sigh once more and glance back out to sea, where the minarets of Scyless glimmer in the sunlight. I kiss my fingertips once and blow, smiling at the silly fancy that Elouise might be standing on a balcony, feeling the touch of my lips in the breeze passing hers.

CHAPTER FIVE

Two days later, we're gathered around a cookfire when Killeen announces that we are visiting Sedaryne, the minor barony of our patron, Baron Tintache, before we make our way to Pastira.

Even Delina groans. "We have our letter for the King, don't we? Why do we need to go see our patron?"

"We need his support, and a letter from him to the King will help, not hinder." Killeen says, snippily. He shoots me a suspicious look. Ah yes, there it is: he's not sure he believes the letter even exists. I'd roll my eyes, but I'd rather not be dodging his hard hands tonight. I wonder if he's even thought about the fact that he'd be less worried now if he'd just leave me the fuck alone.

Melia nods, sending him a warm smile. Weak. "I like visiting the Baron," she says, and over this, I *do* roll my eyes. "We're so lucky to have an aristocrat like him as our patron. Well, it's not really luck. You've worked so cleverly to win his protection and regard." She blinks at Killeen innocently and I can barely keep the incredulity from my face.

But the sycophancy works. Killeen's gaze turn warm, and as he rises to collect a bottle from a cupboard on the outside of his caravan, he drops a hand heavy onto her head. Almost a blessing. She smiles up at him, and my gut turns over.

I glance around at the group. Stemen's expression is steady. He's always ready to back me, and I'm glad of it, but he's not sensitive to these kinds of dynamics. Probably thinks I'm reactive.

But Joseph's eyes are on me, and I wonder if I've given away too much of my thoughts. But if I have, he's not inclined to reprimand: he quirks an eyebrow at me, and I send him a small grin. He returns it, offering a visible, almost stage-worthy heaving sigh that makes me chuckle low. Another who wishes Melia would stop playing to Killeen's already over-inflated ego. Maybe he'd be less inclined to be expecting the world - and me - on a platter, if he wasn't flattered by those who actually know him well.

"Something entertaining you, Liv?" Delina says sharply, a malicious light in her eye.

"Your face," I say flatly.

"Liv. Keep a civil tongue in your head, or I'll put it there for you," Killeen says threateningly, settling onto the log beside me. Of course he chooses to sit next to me. In reach. My skin prickles.

"Oh you will, will you?" I murmur into the mug of soup I'm making my way through, unable to let it slide.

"What do you think the Baron will like to see?" Pearlene sends me a significant look, and I subside irritably.

"The children always love a good tumbling act," Joseph says, and when I glance at him, he's also communicating that I should be keeping my mouth shut. "But the Baron likes something more adult for after they've found their ways to bed."

"I'm surprised you're not volunteering to revisit your interlude as Sarine," Delina says innocently. "You do seem to enjoy playing the jade."

I curl my lip at her and don't deign to respond.

"It's not the role, with Liv," Melia says, smiling at me warmly. "Whatever she puts her mind to, she's exceptional at. Jade or queen."

"She's got the skills," Killeen says, his dark eyes on my face, and I know I'm meant to be grateful, even moved by his positive regard. He runs a hand along the length of my thigh and I have to work hard not to twitch away. But I know if I do, anger will follow. I hate these choices. "And the kind of looks that manage to be beautiful no matter the character. It's part of what makes her a good player."

I force myself to give him a gracious smile as if in thanks. My gut curdles as I do. Every compliment is just another move on the orlan board with him. Strings attached to everything. As if to prove it, he slides his hand toward my inner thigh. I suppress the desire to shove him away, but anger is banked like a fire in my bones.

Stemen glances at Killeen's grasping touch on my knee, stirs, and leans forward. Ready to distract. "Should we do our snippets and excerpts show? We're only visiting for a night or two, right? Maybe this is our chance to get a sense of what Sedaryne would like, for next time we visit." He offers the bottle back to Killeen, not reaching too much so that Killeen has to release my leg to take it. Relief is almost like joy, and I hate that I feel so trapped that even him letting me go feels like so good.

"Poetry and a few teasers to give them a taste?" Pearlene nods, takes the offered bottle from Killeen, sips and extends it to Joseph. "I like it. It takes some doing, with the costume changes, but it would set us up for next season."

"If we come back," Killeen says. Joseph refuses the bottle, and Pearlene swiftly hands it back to Killeen, before he can grab at my body again. He drinks deep, and adds, "We might be the Royal Theatrical Troupe by then, and bound to Pastira. And Baron Tintache will have to make do with Picton or one of the other mid-range troupes."

"You think we could win, truly?" Melia turns wide, impressed eyes to Killeen, and I feel nauseous. I can feel the shift in his body, the loosening that results from her ingratiation. Why does she bind herself to him? Can she not see the risk? Can she not see how he uses the choice between his anger and his ego to make it seem like the safest bet is let him have what he wants? And how much she winds up giving him unwilling as a result?

"We're strong. At least strong enough to be competition," Pearlene says.

"And then we'll be rich. Richer than we've ever seen," Delina puts in. Is it really true? I can feel the longing in my bones. Wealth means stability. Security. And the ability to have my own way.

"We'd all be able to retire on the amount we'd earn in that year," Killeen says, and I hate that my body resonates with an echo of the yearning I hear in his voice. "Enough that we could sell our vans and buy a house, so long as it's outside the capital. But we need to win it first." His gaze rests on me, and there's a slow burning desire sitting behind it. It feels like a throw-back to when we first met, in some ways. Before the ugliness of his possessiveness made itself clear to me, and colored everything that came after. Actual desire, not just injured entitlement. The crawl of it over my skin is like spiders, now, and my heartbeat kicks up in panic.

"Well, all we can do is our best," Pearlene says, in a tone sharp enough to draw his gaze off me. I'm grateful for it.

Joseph's expression is sympathetic when I make myself look around. "And prepare as much as we can," he adds quietly. The sense that he knows what I'm feeling is unsettling, but I'm also grateful that he seems to have my back. Maybe I've been too worried about him seeing through me; maybe he's another I can keep at my back, like Stemen.

"That means bed for me," Stemen says quickly. "I need my rest."

"Me too," I say, grateful for the out. I rise, and the loss of Killeen's cloying warmth beside me feels like freedom for a moment. "I'm for bed. Sleep well, everyone." I hasten across the circle to my caravan, give them all a final wave and a smile, and lock the door behind me.

It's almost entirely dark before we roll into Sedaryne, two days later. At sunset, Melia had dashed from wagon to van, lighting the lanterns on their corners so that we didn't smash into one another as the darkness fell. I'm weary and glad that Dragon, as ever, knows his business.

On the far side of the little village, the portcullis on the squat stone keep rattles up in greeting. Killeen guides his two-horse team into the courtyard while the rest of us pull up in a clearing in the thick bush, against the west wall. "Good to see you all again!" Four of the guards emerge from the darkness. "The ostlers will unhitch yon beasties and get them cared for and fed. You go in and get your meal." The man who's speaking looks vaguely familiar and he gives me a broad grin that fades a little at the expression on my face.

I slip inside my caravan and dab carmine across the round of my lips, and buff a series of dots into my cheeks. It'll have to do. I grab a leather satchel from a cupboard above my bed and make to shove into it the two scrolls Elouise had entrusted me with.

As I do, I see that she's wrapped a piece of paper around the two together, tied with rough jute string. I frown and look closer, setting my lantern down on the table. My suggestion would be to keep these in your possession at all times, her gracious hand reads. No doubt some would see the contents of one as treachery, and if the other were in his possession, he would have no further need of you.

Ice trickles through my veins. This is a risk I hadn't considered, but she's right. I send gratitude off into the night, wishing I'd said more while we were still at Scyless. I add a scarf and woolen hat to the scrolls, hoping the chill on the air will be sufficient explanation for the bag.

Melia is waiting for me at the bottom of the steps down from my caravan. "Didn't you... spend time with him?" Melia asks hesitantly, nodding her head subtly in the direction of the young man who'd greeted us.

"Oh!" I glance back over my shoulder. "You know, you might be right!" I slide my arm through her elbow. "I'd forgotten. Clearly not that memorable, I guess!"

Melia looks at me like I've been terribly cruel. I shrug. "It's good that you got the letter. To the king I mean," she says, as if feeling her way into a conversation.

"The duchess is generous," I say, smiling. "She always has been."

"She always is," Melia replies slowly. "But that's a precious document. Wouldn't it be better in Killeen's safe? In his caravan?"

The ice is back in my veins. "Reckon it'll be fine. I'll keep it safe," I say brusquely, releasing her arm. Fucking Killeen. Why does Melia keep making herself his lapdog? I stride out more swiftly ahead of her into the golden light pouring from the open doors of the keep.

Inside, a maid greets us and conducts us directly into a large hall. The Baron sits at the head of a U-shaped table, a ramshackle cluster of children arrayed down one side, laughing and crying and generally carrying on at the top of their lungs.

Killeen is already at the Baron's left hand, stroking his mustache as he always does and talking animatedly to his patron. He adores power but it intimidates him. The Baron is the perfect balance - minor nobility, but with connections. The remnants of the ice in my veins flares to anger as I watch him smirk through the conversation with the Baron, but I school my features carefully.

To the Baron's right is a woman I've never seen on any of our previous visits. Auburn curls cascade about her shoulders and acres of creamy white bosom are on display. She's stunning and out of place, like a true gem amongst cut glass jewels. And she looks... bored. Little wonder: the Baron is completely ignoring her.

"Who's she?" I waylay a maid carrying a tray of drinks, and claim a red wine at the same time.

"Baroness Erindon, the Baron's new wife," she reports, and her lip curls a little as she adds, "Thinks she's too good for us lowly country folk. And her not even from a titled family!"

"I see," I murmur. Erindon sighs visibly, her pillowy lips parting prettily, and the Baron distractedly waves a maid to refill her already-full glass.

Killeen, still talking to the Baron, narrows his eyes at me. I raise my brows questioningly, channeling innocence. He scowls and I grin a little maliciously. Don't fucking tempt me, you controlling fuck.

I weave my way between people and make Joseph move down so I can settle onto the bench that runs down the left arm of the U, barely two empty seats away from the gorgeous woman. I make a little fuss as I wedge myself into the spot, as if Joseph has been reluctant to move, and it's enough to draw her attention. Her eyes - green-blue like the sea - fall on me briefly. They're heavy-lidded, and I smile at her, the slow secret smile I know is like a promise. She double-takes, her own echoing smile bemused.

It's enough. The frisson of the chase fizzes in my veins. And why not? Because of Killeen? I'm not going to let him dictate what I do. Fuck that. I left obedience in the dust with Isharin. I set my own guiding star now.

Without dropping her gaze, I touch the tip of my tongue to my bottom lip and then scrape my teeth over the round of it. I drop my head to one side, letting my smile be a question to her, as if not sure why she's watching me. She blinks twice and then looks away, a light flush creeping up her cheeks.

"Gods, Liv." Joseph, beside me, blows out a breath, impressed. "Is that a good idea?"

I give a low, gut-deep chuckle as I turn to meet slightly worried gray eyes. "Probably not," I agree cheerfully. I wrinkle my nose at him, my grin lop-sided. "But I've never let what's wise get in the way of what I want."

Joseph raises a single brow and returns my grin. "Well, that's a motto to live by," he murmurs, and raises his glass to me.

"Or die by, I suppose," I say, laughing. I clink my wine with his, casting just a quick glance at the Baroness. She's watching me out of the corner of her eye, but she's suddenly sitting upright. The extraordinary curve of her breasts are just subtly pressed forward, the tie of her chemise cutting in a little. No one else would notice but I do. The shift of posture betrays all I need to know.

And she doesn't look bored anymore.

The meal is delicious, and my skin is coming alive, feeling her gaze tracing over me as I eat and chatter with Joseph. He's entertained to be made part of my show, but if he grins just a little broader than usual, she probably doesn't even notice. I let my eyes drift to her often enough to keep her wondering who I am, and why I'm here.

And then I rise from the table as the meal is being cleared. I pat at my mouth with a white napkin before I turn away, letting my gaze linger on her over my shoulder.

"Be careful," Joseph says.

"Careful?" My lips curve as I smile down at him "Maybe."

He shakes his head, chuckling airily to himself. I let my hips swing loose as I make my way to a dim hallway. I'm not even sure where it leads, except that it's not where the dishes of food have been carted to and from. Hopefully private enough.

As soon as I'm out of sight of the great hall, I lean back against the wall. Swiftly, I tuck my hands into my bodice, arrange my breasts and tighten the laces just a little. The work of a moment, but it's done just in time.

"I..." The Lady Erindon wears a very pretty blush. "I didn't..." Her gaze dips to the swell of my breasts showing above the bodice and the fizz in my veins slows to a rolling boil.

She's mine.

"Hello. I... I'm Liv. I just wanted a little quiet, but... now I don't know where I'm going." I laugh self-deprecatingly.

"Erindon... T-the hall can be noisy," she offers hesitantly. She nibbles at her bottom lip. "I could... would the library be quiet enough?"

I let my gaze rest on hers for a long moment, and the flush renews itself. "You are stunning, my lady, did you know?" I murmur in a low voice, almost inaudible.

She leans towards me as if she can't quite make out my words, those glorious lips parting. I nearly lean towards her, press my mouth to hers, but I know she's not ready for that. Nearly. But we're too close to her husband still.

I clear my throat as if embarrassed. It's the last thing I am, but a little bashfulness can do wonders. "I... my apologies, my lady, I... But yes, sorry, yes, a library would be perfect."

"Of course. I would hate for you to find our hospitality lacking," she says, and sets off down the hallway ahead of me. Her hips are rolling, her backside round and pinching into a slender waist barely a hand's width across. Fuck. The warmth unfurling low in my gut is better than drinking.

"It's been a long trip," I say, to keep the silence at bay as we walk. And I blather on about nothing as I follow her. And then she pauses at a door, her eyes on me, and her color suddenly hectic. I stand a little too close. Her breathing comes short, lips parted, and her pupils dilate as she tries the handle twice before she succeeds at turning it.

And as soon as it opens, I follow her through it in a rush, spinning her and pressing my body against hers so that her back shoves the door closed. Her breath goes ragged, her hands rising to my hips as I curve my fingers in a caress from temple to chin, sliding a hand under the glory of her hair. I stare into her eyes, a bare inch between our lips. "I..." she starts, then trails off.

"You are extraordinary," I whisper, running a thumb over her bottom lip. She makes a sound I can't place, but her head leans into my hand. "Gods."

"Gods, please."

Fuck. How am I meant to resist anything like this?!

My mouth meets hers, and after a moment of slow discovery, she moans in the back of her throat and her hand tangles in my dark curls. She turns my mouth up to hers and plunders it with surprising passion.

This is no innocent.

I love finding secret sapphics amongst the aristocracy.

I slide her chemise away from that creamy expanse of skin, swear softly and kiss a long line across the naked flesh from the sensitive skin of her neck and down the gorgeous curve of her breast. I dip my tongue below the line of her shirt and she gasps, hands slamming against the door as I swirl my tongue against her nipple.

I pull the tie on her chemise, reach behind her to yank loose the bow knotted there and give one rough tug downward at the front of her stays. I close my lips around her nipple and suckle, not gently, and she moans deep, her head falling back against the door. She grips a fist in the hair at the back of my head. Desire whips up in my chest at the minor restraint.

Obediently, I work at it until her nipple is swollen and pink and she's panting. And then I switch to the other, plucking gently at the first with my thumb. I take a moment to stare at her, beautiful and disheveled, her eyelids heavy. "Please," she whispers. "He cannot... I need..."

I smile, enjoying her desperation. "I think we're missing dessert." There's a moment of hesitation, like she's suddenly realizing what she's doing, but before it can take hold, I drop to my knees before her. "I want something sweet," I murmur, grinning up at her wickedly as I slide my hands up her legs, raising all the layers of skirts.

Her thighs are round and soft and made to be kissed. So I do, slowly working my way up as her legs separate, the only sound in the quiet library her ragged breathing. I drive my nose into the soft curls between her legs, and she gasps even at that. I slide gentle fingers along the slick of her lips. She's soaked, and I smile triumphantly to myself.

"Yes, alright, fuck, I want you. Would you do it already?"

My chuckle surprises us both, but I'm not one to keep a woman waiting. Much.

I slide my tongue from her sex to the rise of her clit and latch, lashing my tongue against it. She cries out, a loud sound in the quiet of the castle, and I grin to myself. She stretches out arms to either side, gripping at a shelf. I slide two fingers to her entrance, and her breathing gets even more hectic. She groans, a guttural sound as I drive them into her, and she sinks towards me, like her legs have given away.

She dislodges a book and it falls with a loud smack to the floor.

I curl my fingers deep inside her slick heat, once, and again, finding the ridges that I know will have her coming in a matter of minutes.

Her cries are taking on a rhythm, and I reach up over her skirts to grip her hand. I lift it to her own rosy nipples, and I can hear the shift in her pleasure as she begins to pinch at them.

Her sex is clutching at me now, and I set to her clit with a will. We don't need to be caught in the act, and dessert must be already served.

Her hands slide down, gripping briefly at my head and then they slide further down and I moan against her as her fingers slide inside my bodice, and my nipples, already roused, reach aching hardness swiftly.

And every muscle inside her body clenches a split second before she cries aloud one long last time, her sex gripping me tight, followed by fluttery ripples at my fingers. I lash her clit harder, her fingers pinch tight at my nipples and she slides down the door towards me.

It's difficult not to be dislodged but I've done this enough to know how to catch a woman as she's coming and lower her gently to the floor. I keep at it until I can feel the ebb of the orgasm drifting from her flesh.

Her body is loose and pliant as I withdraw, drawing her skirts down. I pause above her, just watching her as the afterglow fades, as she comes back to herself, her breathing slowing. Her chemise is rumpled, the ties trailing across her bared breasts, her stays awkwardly shoved down. She cracks an eyelid at me, and I smile.

"That smile…" she murmurs. "That smile is dangerous."

I grin. "This?"

"Well," she says, still dazed, pulling the fallen book out from under her hair, "all of this is." She gestures at my whole body. "You are truly… And with that smile as well…" she trails off, reaching out to draw me to her. She kisses me thoroughly, and palms my breast, pinching the nipple between thumb and forefinger beneath the cloth of my bodice. I swallow the sound in my throat. "What if I wanted my own dessert?" She says with a pout.

I smile again, raise a playful brow. "I'd never stand in milady's way."

She laughs. "I would love to know what sounds you make…" she murmurs. "That would… sustain me, for a time. Just give me a minute."

"Take your time," I reply. "Though… is there a lock to this door?"

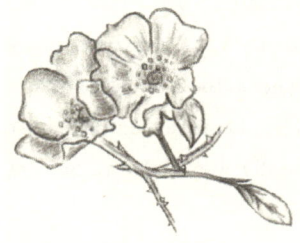

CHAPTER SIX

I wake in my own caravan to Killeen's bellow.

He does not sound happy. He bellows again, but it's not the usual up-and-at-'em yell he offers of a morning. That's usually cheerful. This isn't. I throw myself out of bed, clambering swiftly into skirts and bodices, then shoving my feet into boots. If it's me he's angry at, I need to be ready.

I emerge into the bright sunlight to find ostlers leading horses from the keep. They look serious, and I gulp as I close the door behind me.

"Perhaps not the best choice you've ever made, Liv," Delina says cattily, as she passes, leading her horse to her caravan.

"Me?" I ask innocently. "What have I done?"

Stemen shakes his head at me, looking almost disgusted. That stings, more than I'd like to admit. Joseph's mouth is tight with regret, his gaze a warning.

Fuck.

Finally catching sight of me, Killeen roars, "Decided to fucking join us, did you? Fucking self-absorbed fucking brat."

"Picton would tell you profanity is no replacement for poetry," I say, somewhere between defensive and airy. "I don't know what I'm meant to have done, but as you can see, I've been deeply busy for hours—sleeping!"

"Are you going to tell me you didn't fuck the baron's wife?" He bellows the words, and even as panic spears my guts, my mind already is reminding me the heat of his fury is a relief. Cold, implacable anger scares me far, far more than this fiery display. But fuck.

The truth is only going to hurt me. And her. And she's not here right now, and I am.

And letting him have this would be dangerous in a thousand ways. If he wins anything from me, it'll be the beginning of having to gracefully acquiesce. It would make having to fuck him more likely, and I cannot bear the thought of it.

"The baron's wife?" I play for time, echoing his words, disbelieving, then inject scorn into my voice. "What—when exactly would I have had time to do that?"

"You both left the table during dessert," he yells, stalking slowly closer. The troupe gathers a safe distance away.

I edge down the steps. I'll need to be on the flat if he decides to belt me. "Did we? I needed some air, so I went to find some. Joseph saw me leave! Did I leave with the baron's wife, Joseph?"

"No," he agrees reluctantly. He hates being drawn into conflict like this, and he knows that even if I left the hall before she did, she definitely followed me. I'm leaning on his goodwill toward me, and he doesn't like it. Well, he doesn't have to, so long as he only tells the truth I've asked for.

"See?" I say triumphantly. I tap a finger to my lips. "I did hear from one of the maids that she's not well liked. Said she thought she was too good for a little backwater like this."

"A backwater?!" Killeen's nose is purpling. I've stung his pride as well now. He likes to believe Baron Tintache is an important figure at court. I could kick myself—an obvious misstep. I blame the lack of morning maté.

"She was quoting the baroness, I think," I add hastily. "I think it's why they don't like her. Probably some maid with a vendetta against her mistress, telling stories."

He stares at me, his black eyes hard. His voice is low—almost too low to be heard—as he says, "Y'know, Liv, once upon a time I might've believed you. Probably would've. But now, after all the time you've spent playing me..." He shakes his head disdainfully. "I can't believe a word that comes out of that pretty fucking mouth anymore." He sounds almost sad, behind the bitter belligerence.

I toss my head. "Believe what you like," I say, performing the exact degree of anger I'd be displaying if he really had accused me when I hadn't done anything wrong.

And I *haven't* done anything wrong. Acting on desire is never the problem. The problem is men thinking they get to rule women. The problem is men getting offended that some women won't choose them, or won't choose fidelity. The problem is the stupidity of having beautiful, passionate women like Erindon bound to backwaters and boring old men and expecting her to suck it up and put his wishes—wishes born of ego and a desire to dominate—above her own.

Unlike certain others, I've never sought to force anyone to fuck me, and frankly, that puts me one up on Killeen before the weighing of sins even starts. "I've done nothing to warrant this kind of treatment. I pull my weight. I draw crowds. I take only my share, and I don't screw anyone else over. I deserve to be treated with respect!"

Killeen's face turns ugly, his upper lip curling as if I were less than manure beneath his boot. Fucking arsehole. Then he opens his mouth. "Respect is earned," he hisses. "And you want to claim you didn't make promises with your fucking cunt to get me to take you on?" He steps closer, and I quash the instinct to recoil and retreat, instead raising my gaze to his. My gut swirls into nausea. Fearless—I need to look fearless. He's like a dog. Stare him down.

"Any promises you think I made are in your gods-be-damned head, Killeen," I say, every word bitten off, and I'm proud that there's not even a quaver in my voice. I glare at him, chin high. "My cunt doesn't speak for me. If you were unhappy with our deal, you should've said. We shook and we signed, and there was nothing in that contract about being your fucking jade. Keep your fantasies between you and your hand and stop projecting them into our arrangement."

His eyes bug out, and I know I've pushed him too far. He draws his arm back and backhands me across the face. The pain spears through my cheek, and it feels like he's split the skin. I yelp, dodging away from another blow and falling against the steps of my own caravan.

Another blow doesn't come.

When I turn back, Stemen is holding Killeen's arm. The blond man is far stronger than Killeen, but the unbridled fury on Killeen's face makes me shrink. "Stop this," Stemen says. "Stop it now. You cannot come in with accusations like this and expect her not to retaliate."

I spit blood into the grass, but when I run my tongue over them, no teeth are loose.

"As if she *didn't* fuck that fat cow," Delina chimes in snidely. "She's never seen a cunt she doesn't want."

"Except yours, perhaps, Delina?" Joseph's tone is mild. Delina spits on the ground, her mouth an ugly moue.

"This isn't how we do things," Pearlene says, her voice quavering. Stemen drops Killeen's arm as soon as he stops struggling. "You can't beat on your troupe, Killeen. You want her to leave, now? Right when you've finally got a way in with the king thanks to her?"

"She's probably lying about that too," Delina says cattily. "Can't see how she's not."

I draw myself upright. "I have the fucking letter right here. Tempted to torch it, after this display of banality." Two letters—one an impossible promise I'm starting to think is the only way I'll find out of this contract with Killeen.

Killeen's face goes white with some combination of fury and horror. "You think she doesn't have it?" He turns to Delina, and his voice is pure consternation. It's perversely satisfying.

Melia's anxious voice cuts through. "Of course she has it. Don't you, Liv?"

"Yeah. I have it," I say, looking down my nose at Killeen.

"I want it now," Killeen says suddenly. "It belongs in my safe."

"No fucking way."

Joseph steps forward, and his voice is firm, but I can see the tremor in his hand. "You cannot expect her to hand over that letter when you've just hit her, Killeen," he says reasonably.

"She threatened to burn it!" Killeen protests. "And this isn't some kind of Rover clan, where everyone gets a say. I'm the fucking boss here."

Stemen's mouth tightens, and when he speaks, his voice rumbles in his chest. "I won't be part of a troupe where skilled players are beaten on," he says. "So you'd best work on getting your temper under control if you'd like to keep us all."

Killeen glances around as if to check whether everyone agrees. Joseph looks uncharacteristically mulish, Pearlene's jaw is set, and Melia looks terrified. Delina is the only one grinning and shaking her head.

"But if she burns it..." he wheedles helplessly.

"Someone else can keep it safe," Melia says in a tiny voice, flinching when Killeen turns his furious gaze on her.

"Joseph," I say swiftly. "He can hang onto it 'til Pastira."

Joseph is like velvet and steel. He seems weak to some, but he's not, and Killeen's one of those who underestimate him. There's been more than a handful of times he's mocked Joseph for enjoying being fucked, implying it makes him less of a man. Killeen knows nothing of the strength required to let a cock take you like that.

"Fine, Joseph," Killeen agrees, and I know he's thinking he could pressure Joseph at the drop of a hat.

Joseph gives me a steady, sardonic look, then says, "Very well. But let me tell you, Killeen, that if you try to get rid of Liv before we reach Pastira, or if you force her to sleep with you... that letter will disappear, along with more than half your troupe."

"We wouldn't win the king's approval without her anyway," Pearlene puts in, half placating and half matter of fact, before Killeen can say something else to decimate the remnants of the troupe.

"Right." Stemen scans us each in turn. "Now, can we get out of here?"

"The baron gave us an hour to be off his land," Melia reminds everyone.

I bite my tongue against the question I want to ask and slip inside the caravan to fetch the letter. As I untie the rough jute that binds the two scrolls together, tears flood into my eyes. It's just the aftermath—the shock of it, I tell myself. But I hand the scroll off to Joseph without meeting his eyes, then hasten back to my own van.

My fingers are clumsy and my vision blurred as I strap Dragon into the harness. But as the caravans roll out, I settle into the driver's seat, a giant hat tied beneath my chin. It shields my face—both from the sun and from the gaze of others.

I'm used to hiding my tears. No one will see this weakness.

CHAPTER SEVEN

The weeks spent crossing the country are relatively conflict-free, leaving me to weigh the pathways before me. I avoid Killeen as much as is possible without appearing to be avoiding him, while he restricts himself to dark gazes from under his brows across the campfire at night. The rest of the troupe works hard at keeping things calm, and for the most part, they succeed. I'd be grateful, but I'm too annoyed at Killeen for creating the problem in the first place. I can't help but hope that Elouise's promise of writing letters to people in Pastira who might assist in creating the first woman-led troupe will bear fruit. I don't like relying on others for such things, but there's little I can do until we arrive. Maybe then I can work out whether there's way to make it real. I need to make it real.

I'm sitting on the driving bench at the front of my caravan, watching Dragon's haunches, when the haze on the horizon resolves into the humping low line of the capital. My gut drops, like the moment when I throw myself out into space during a tumbler's routine, and wait to be caught.

Or to slam into the ground.

This was once home.

And then my mouth floods with bitterness. It was never home.

Home is meant to be safe. Secure. Where you're loved. Where no one will ever threaten you. That's the story we tell in almost all of our plays - the hero ventures out into the world, and by the time they return home, all the repetitive ordinariness has become endearingly safe, like a warm embrace. They are welcomed with tears and love, and everyone has learned to appreciate their idiosyncrasies.

Not Pastira.

My heartbeat is thudding hard in my ears, and I force myself to draw a slow breath, to steady myself.

I glance down, and my knuckles are white on the reins. The breath shudders into my lungs, and with a swoop in my middle, every hard-won mote of self-worth shivers and dissipates.

As if it never was.

I'm eleven again, shaking in too few clothes as the curtain rises and reveals an audience of eyes staring at me. Fear judders through me as the bidding starts, and I realize the full horror that Isharin has knowingly sent me into. Terror clutches at me, chill hands scouring at my shoulders. I yank up my sleeve, not sure if I'm still standing on that filthy stage, and dig my nails into my forearm.

The pain jerks me back into the present, and I'm panting, bent double in my seat.

"Liv?" Melia is on horseback for a change, and she pulls up alongside my caravan, concern writ large on her face. "Are you well?"

"Fine." I force a smile, and gods in heaven, I know that despite everything, it's convincing.

This is what's saved me. Making believe.

"Oh, good," she says, uncertainly. "I hope... you're from Pastira, right?"

I nod silently, my chest aching with the effort of keeping my breath even when I feel like I can't get enough air. "It's been a while," I say, and my voice is remarkably calm. "I would guess some has changed."

"No doubt," she murmurs. "But no family to see? No friends? Surely there must be some you knew here?"

There were. And they either left me, or I left them behind to save myself. I dig my nails into my palm this time - less obvious, but still effective. The shadow recedes again.

"Oh sure," I say, perfectly casual. "Well, no family anymore, but I suppose there would be some of my old friends." Fucking Isharin's face, still floating across my vision, even all these years after he fucked me over. "But it's been a long time. I doubt they'd even recognize me."

"Really? It's been so long? You're a pretty memorable person," she says with that shy smile that sets my teeth on edge. Too much sweetness. Manipulation, every time. I can't blame her for it - gods know I've played half the world to get this far from that filthy stage - but I'm almost positive that I'm more convincing. It's agonizing to see through the play and still have to pretend it's effective. Memorable person, she says...

I laugh, and am almost shocked at how sincerely light-hearted it sounds. "I was a child, though. None of the memorable stuff." I wink, giving a little shimmy of my shoulders, and predictably she flushes. I enjoy her discomfort. "I guess we'll find out. Or maybe not - surely we'll be mostly at the palace?"

"That's true," she replies, biting her lip in thought. "Killeen is keen to get the letter in front of the King and Queen as soon as he can."

"So are we going straight to the palace to present ourselves? No lingering in the city?"

"It seems that way." She clears her throat. "Liv, you know that we can't do this without you, right? You're... you're likely one of the best players Rescalin has seen - ever! And I... I know Killeen is annoying. I get it, I promise. But it's not just about him. We're all..." She trails off as I turn a weary look on her. "I just... this could be huge. For all of us. The money, alone..."

Irritation fills my chest, almost like anger. Does she really think I don't recognize how much money this could bring?! Can she not see how much I've already put on the table to bet on this future? I close my eyes for a moment, gathering strength, before I reply, and when I open them, she's almost cowering. I try to keep my voice from being harsh but it sounds almost brittle as a result. "Sure. I get it, Melia, I do, I swear. But I'm also not going to let Killeen use the possibility of all of that to manipulate me into fucking him."

I give her a direct look, and she almost flinches from it. "I have worked too fucking hard to get to a place where I choose who I fuck. To make what I want my guiding star. And if I let him manipulate me into it now..." My voice turns more gravelly than I'd ever have intended. It's almost a betrayal. I can't have this gentle soul seeing through my masks. It might end me. I clear my throat and shake my head, aiming for matter-of-fact. "It'll mean that all of that work was for nothing."

"I... I'm sorry he can't seem to leave it be," she says hesitantly, looking down at her hands on the reins. "I think it's beyond actual... like I'm not clear he actually wants it anymore. It's just his pride."

I raise a single brow. "Indeed. It's not desire. If it was desire, he'd give a fuck about what I want."

Melia pinches her lips between her teeth for a moment, as if this is too much for her to take. "I... I think he does, in a way," she says slowly. "But..."

"I don't really give a rat's arse about untangling it, anymore," I say with a shrug. "Like you said, he's more interested in his pride than in me, so whatever care might sit alongside that counts for shit, frankly."

She nods jerkily, and gives me a tight smile as she presses her heels to her steed. She knows it's fair. Gods, I'd bet even Killeen knows it's fair. Just can't get beyond his ego.

The exchange has at least given me an out for some of the fear and sadness the sight of Pastira had roused in me - even if it came out as snippy-ness and anger and performance. And now, when I raise my eyes to where the road rumbles up to the red-painted gate, the thick-layered emotions are locked back up, tightly controlled.

The soldiers on the gate cheer, as they often do when a players' troupe arrives, wherever we go, and I stand briefly to curtsy deeply, then grin and wave at them. Never hurts to draw the eye of the crowd, and gods know we might fail horribly with the King and need to turn to the city for coin. These guards will be better for disseminating news of our arrival than hiring a crier or sending running boys to pin up posters.

There's a whoop as Delina flips her skirts up briefly, and a roar as Stemen tugs his shirt off to display his finely-sculpted chest and arms. I know the routine almost as well as I know the back of my own hand.

We trundle through the city, and I hide the way that memories of every corner keep gut-punching me and stealing my breath. I'd thought it had been long enough, but perhaps it never would be.

Here's the corner where I had begged for coin with my mother before she died when I was four. There by a fountain is the cluster of children - I'd been one of them, once - congregated together for safety and in the hope of yet more coin. The mouth of a street that ended in an alleyway where I'd been robbed by four older children. They'd taken the silver coin I'd been given by a lady enamoured of my eyes' shade of green, and the stub of bread her companion had tossed me. I'd been six then. I've worked hard to leave those days behind.

We pass the market, and the familiar smell of rotting banana and native plums fills my nostrils, and I know it's because a wagon is parked in a back alley for the refuse and mouldering produce the storekeepers hadn't been able to sell in time. I know because I remember rooting through it for edible scraps. Now I have enough money that I'm more likely to have an upset belly over the richness of my dessert than my food turning sour.

We pass The Kettle's Song, a pub where Isharin had liked to spend his evenings, and I gulp and look away. I don't need to see whether he's there, with some other child's trusting hand in his. My stomach turns over, and in my mind I clutch at the shoulders of that eleven year old version of me, telling her not to give in to the devastation, and that his betrayal means everything about him and not about her - about me. And repeating, over and over, that things get better.

That we make them better.

It's a relief when we cross into the part of the city where the aristocracy live - arrayed below the palace like her skirts. This part is less familiar, though I'd visited it occasionally with Isharin when he had a heist of some kind or another. I'd often stood watch while he snuck in and ransacked whatever mansion we were paid to burgle.

Sometimes he'd emerged with jewels and gemstones that too swiftly had to be handed over for our pay - and sometimes he carried only scrolls or folded pieces of paper. At the time, I'd thought it was ludicrous that someone could pay so much money for a slip of paper. Now, I occasionally wondered what precious secrets we'd handed over that must've been worth more than material goods.

In a way, seeing how the aristocracy lived was part of what had saved me - knowing what wealth looked like. What could be. What money made possible.

But I'd learned, too, that money wasn't enough to earn my own way. No; Isharin's betrayal had taught me that when it came down to it, it was everyone for themselves, and that no amount of believing in justice was going to mean anyone gave me what I wanted. Or even what I needed. Only I could do that, and I learned to do whatever I had to to make sure I got it.

The Pastiran streets make me feel like I'm a knife's edge from being eleven and at the mercy of those who don't care who they hurt. But as we rattle up to the red-painted gates, the distance from eleven reasserts itself, the tension in my gut slowly settling. But finally, we leave all the memories behind, and approach the palace itself. My chest loosens like I've been wearing a corset bound too tight and someone has cut the laces.

Killeen, straightening his striped waistcoat and twirling his mustache nervously, approaches the guards on the gate. Joseph, giving me a significant look, trails behind him, Elouise's scroll in his hand.

I swallow, thinking of the other scroll secreted in my caravan. I hadn't really thought about how I might wrangle this part of the plan. How to get the scroll into the King's hands without Killeen or anyone else knowing? I frown briefly, then clear my gaze deliberately as the guards conduct us through the gates and into a large courtyard, offering a smile to those left on the gate.

We're led from here into a smaller courtyard with a tree in the center. The guard nods. "You'll have to wait here while we ask the Convenor of Royal Arts whether the royal family is interested in seeing you perform, and in you being included in the competition. The Duchess is the King's cousin, but that's not a guarantee. If they are, you'll be given lodgings here in the palace. But if not, you'll have to leave."

He gives us all an appraising look. "I'll arrange for refreshments to be brought - and water so that you can clean up a bit. The Convenor is a fastidious type. You'll want to look your best." He hesitates once more. "It may be some time."

Killeen thanks him for his consideration, barely hiding his consternation at not having known the protocol. "Should we be in costume?" Pearlene asks, her brow creased. "Fancy clothes at least, no?"

"Yes. Ready the clothing for after you've bathed though." Killeen looks at me for a long moment, and there's a vulnerability there that disgusts me somehow. I realize that he's not been sure whether the letter was real and now this is something like guilt or gratitude.

I turn from his wordless gaze before the bitterness I owe Isharin can boil over my lips at him, and stride up the steps into my caravan. It's all I can do to keep my lip from curling, but I'm sure Melia's happy with my performance.

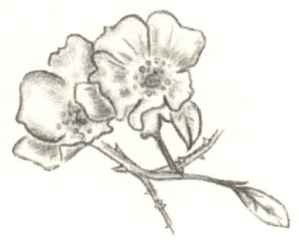

CHAPTER EIGHT

"The King and Queen would like to see you," the guard tells Killeen. We've washed and dressed and inhaled the food they've offered, expecting the Convenor to appear at any moment.

We look at each other, wondering what to make of this. "Is there a protocol...?" Killeen asks, almost like a little boy in his uncertainty.

His words trail off as a tall, dark-skinned person with satiny black hair curving to their jaw strides into the courtyard, orange-yellow silks billowing around them. Their gaze is brisk and assessing, then they speak. "It's not usual for the Royal family to approve their visiting players," they say, their voice resonant and deep. "Usually I do that, and select the performers to compete for the position of Royal Theatrical Troupe. But they are disagreeing, currently, about what they want in their entertainment. And so, they have requested that you present yourselves to them."

"For approval to be part of the competition?" Killeen is wide-eyed. You would've thought a player would have more artifice.

The Convenor inclines their head. "Indeed."

"Should we... perform?" Killeen asks them, his uncertainty fully on display. I almost cringe at the sight of it, so naked.

"That is up to you. The Duchess's commendation will have some weight, though they are likely to want some indication of your breadth. But I would recommend that whatever you do, you keep the women clothed as they are." They scour their dark eyes across the four of us. "The Queen feels that Prince Shandor is exposed to too much... voluptuousness in his performers. She may veto if there is too much on display."

I resist the urge to roll my eyes. Does the Queen understand that the Prince will find whatever kind of women he wants - the question is only how. Their gaze rests on me, and I shift uneasily. "We do tumbling and juggling as well. Perhaps that is a better introduction to us," I suggest.

"The Princess would prefer that," the Convenor responds. "Now come."

We hasten after them as they stride loose-limbed through the palace, their silks fluttering. Killeen cannot pull himself together to formulate a plan, so Pearlene and I outline a quick series of short performances: a poem, a tumble, a juggle and finally the death scene from The Player and the Prince. It will offer enough of our skills up for their consideration.

We pause outside large wooden doors. The Convenor spins to face us. "We will call for you. Be ready." They enter the room, guards pulling the door closed before we can get any sense of what is within.

I draw a breath, smoothing my hands down my skirt. Delina is hoisting her chemise higher, to make herself that little bit more decent, while Killeen fitfully twirls his mustache.

And then before we can do anything more, the doors are opened wide, and the guards nod for us to walk in.

I've always wondered how royalty live. Scyless is elegant, and I'd thought it more or less the measure of what luxury wealth might buy.

I was wrong.

There is gold everywhere. My gaze catches on a chandelier, all gold with gemstones - surely they can't be diamonds? - casting the light into rainbows. Great long banners bearing the emblem of their house flutter against the wall. It's surprisingly bright, given it feels like we are buried in the depths of the palace, but I realize abruptly that we must be in the hall that rests at the pinnacle of the palace. Light pours in on two sides through paper, but stained glass windows glow behind the throne.

For there, with a surprising amount of red between them, are the four thrones of the royal family, arrayed on a square wooden dais.

King Aleshir sits in the largest throne squarely in the center of the room, an enormous and ancient carved wooden thing, with dragons and roses and birds intertwined amongst vines. It is fashioned, I realize after a moment, almost like a tree, rising up towards the sky.

His wife, gaze serene and her brow only slightly wrinkled, is seated on a slender throne placed to his right. To his left, a handsome young man with dark, avid eyes, is seated in a smaller version of the giant tree-throne. And to the left of the Prince, a child of barely ten years sits in a smaller throne. She wriggles uncomfortably - the chair doesn't have a cushion - but she pauses mid-wriggle at the sight of us.

After a moment of hesitation, Killeen steps forward and sweeps an enormous bow, the feathered hat scooping low as he does. We automatically array ourselves behind him, and join him in offering our own courtesies.

We hold the position for a long moment, as a guard announces, "Master Redborne Killeen, Theatrical Director, and his troupe."

Killeen rises, and steps to one side. "May I present Pearlene, reciting a poem penned by Lukanon Delphi in honor of his King, some 500 years ago."

Pearlene steps forward and it's a reminder of how vital she is to our crew. She can be unassuming, but in this moment, she commands every eye in the room. It's difficult for even myself to wrench my gaze away - and I am drawing balls from the satin belt around my waist, while Stemen and Joseph and Delina clamber up each other's bodies and begin the tumble.

I toss the balls higher and higher, taking advantage of the high ceilings. And then Killeen tosses his balls into the flow of mine. I pretend I might miss them, my mouth falling open, and I can feel Her Majesty's gaze on me. And then I begin throwing the balls at Killeen, making believe I'm throwing them hard at his head. He catches them and sends them back, and we play at a slow make-up of our pretended conflict. If only the real thing were so easily resolved. The Queen smiles, when I glance towards the family.

The Princess is staring at the tumblers, gaping as Delina climbs up Melia's round frame, and gasping aloud when Delina leaps out into space, Joseph stepping forward to catch her as Stemen grips at Melia as she falls.

The balance so far seems right. The King is watching Pearlene, and as she finishes, he is the first to applaud.

"Thank you, your majesty," Killeen says in his resonant announcing voice. "And now, we have prepared the final scene of The Player and the Prince, a play we would be honored to present to you and your court in its entirety. We believe the scene is moving in and of itself, but we assure you that with the full context of the play, this moment is heartbreaking."

I take up my position opposite Stemen, drawing a breath to pull myself together. I shake out my hair, setting the curls bouncing. I don't like playing this woman; all selfless love and no sense of self preservation.

"This scene takes place at the end of the play. The King, a hard man, has told his son that his lover the player must die, or that he will disown his son and strip him of his title and position." Killeen gestures broadly with his arm, stepping back to let Stemen and myself take center stage.

"Oh my love! You should not have come," Stemen, as the Prince, declares, horror on his face. He does this so well.

"How could I stay away, knowing the trouble that I have brought down on your head?" I throw my hands out, injecting pleading into my voice. I cannot bear this character; subservience even when she's in love. "Can you forgive me? What would it take for your father to forgive you?"

Stemen shakes his head sorrowfully. "He demands that I destroy you. He imagines that you are some fiendish traitor, using my love against the monarchy, and he will not believe otherwise."

"I..." I fall to my knees, pressing my hands together. Killeen has always insisted that I play it this way, but all I can think is that the only women I know who behave like this are those beaten into submission - not those merely in love. "You do not believe me capable of such things, do you?"

"My love, never! I do not know how the revolutionaries could have known about the delivery of grain, intended to feed our soldiers so they might hold the city. He suspects you, but I know that is impossible." Stemen falls to his knees before me, clutching my hands in his. "But now... now I know not what to do. He has demanded that I... not only that I break it off with you, but that I kill you." He sighs, loudly. "He says that if I do not, I am only proving my allegiance lies not with him or with our family, but with the people and the city. And so he will set me aside."

"He will disown you?" I clutch at my heart - yet more melodrama required of me by Killeen. What other choices might I make, if I were in charge? "Oh I have been a harbinger of doom in your life, my love. You must regret the very day that you found me in that playhouse." I bury my head into my hands, letting my shoulders shake.

"Never!" Stemen roars. "He is an old man and his wits are befuddled. He sees evil in every corner. Besides, my love, perhaps this is the opportunity we have been waiting for. Perhaps this is the moment where we can run together into the sunset. Find a farm near a river. Build our lives together. Marry. Have a horde of children. Be... be happy." Stemen wraps his arms around me and I lean back into him. "Leave all of this conflict behind."

"I..." I gently pull away, taking with me the knife from Stemen's belt, and rising to stand. "It sounds like heaven, truly. Like all I have ever dreamed of, all that I can ever imagine wanting. A simple life, where what we choose what rules us, not tradition or duty or power. Freedom... but I cannot. If my death can earn so much for those I love..."

I turn dramatically, putting the point of the blade to my own throat. "What are you doing?" Stemen says, horror threading his voice. He's a good player, even if the material leaves something to be desired.

"I cannot be the reason you lose everything," I stage-whisper, clutching the hilt of the dagger compulsively, almost anxiously. I fought hard for this uncertainty to be displayed. Killeen wanted me gracious and unflinching, but what woman would choose death with no qualms, simply because of a Prince?

"If I must die, what of it? I am a mere player, not a prince like you. I cannot change this world like you can. My death is not so very big a sacrifice."

"No, please, no, my love!"

Stemen lunges towards me, but I swiftly unspiral the red silk from the hilt of the blade, drawing it across my throat and falling to the floor.

"No! Indella, no!" Stemen kneels beside me and wraps his arms around me, clutching me to him. I make my limbs loose, letting my eyes close slowly. He bows his head and then raises it again and bellows to the ceiling, "Why? Blessed heavens, why would you take her from me? She was all that is good in this world..."

I pause for a long moment, the two of us holding our positions, reveling in the hush that I know means the audience is tangled up in the threads of emotion I have laid out for them. Even with the melodrama and terrible writing.

And then I turn, grip Stemen's hand, pull myself to standing, and I curtsy and he bows, both deep.

A smattering of applause echoes from the stage. It's the Princess and the Queen. The Prince wears an expression I can't quite read, his gaze as hungry as when we entered, and the King strokes his short beard thoughtfully.

"Very well, yes, you may perform for the court tonight. But open with something more cheerful."

"And you must choose something less... provocative than The Player and the Prince," the Queen says. "I recall that play and I don't think it appropriate."

The Prince makes a sound and sits forward as if he would speak, but the Queen sends him a quelling look.

The King rises to his feet, striding down the dais and along the broad carpet that marks the center of the room. "You have an exceptional troupe gathered about you, Master Killeen. It takes significant skill to catch the eye of my cousin Duchess Elouise." As he approaches Killeen, he extends a hand.

Killeen takes it and bows low. He seems uncertain about whether he should be kissing the King's ring, so he lingers over his hand and awkwardly long time. The King takes his hand back and a brief frown crosses his expression. I have to stifle a giggle.

"We are selecting a troupe for the Royal Theatrical Troupe at the moment. Many are lining up to present themselves to us, and we are not sure that the quality of all troupes is comparable. But we have high hopes for you. The troupe so named will be richly compensated for remaining in Pastira and performing for us all year round." He raises his head. "And Mistress Livinia Equitor?"

The shock of being named makes me flush and I step forward, taking refuge in another low curtsy. "Her Grace remarks particularly on your skills. I hope that we will see them on full display."

I murmur something inaudible - I'm not even sure what I say, my heart is thudding so loudly in my ears - and he nods once more. "Yes. Give them two evenings this week, Convenor. And then we shall consider again."

We glance sidelong at each other. Was that dismissal?

"Show them to the green Players' suites in the west sector," the Queen adds. "The ones nearest the Harmony Gardens. They must be given a relaxing space, but do not place them near the other competitors. It is best that the troupes do not interact. And show them also where they may rehearse."

The Convenor bows swiftly, and then leads us from the room as the royal family burst into murmured conversation.

CHAPTER NINE

The suite we are conducted to is more sumptuous than anything I've ever seen. Every inch of fabric on cushion and curtain and table runner is embroidered, and we each have a room with a giant bed within. The main common area opens directly into a stair that runs down into a verdant garden, and the scent of flowers wafts through the lace curtains to perfume the air.

As soon as the door closes, I throw myself onto the cushioned length of a chaise longue, and smooth my fingers over the carved wooden flower there. "I could get used to this!" I exclaim.

Killeen gives me a disapproving glare. "Don't start getting above yourself, Liv."

He's annoyed that Elouise mentioned me specifically. But I need his goodwill to make sure whatever plays he selects shows off my skills, so I bite my tongue and play to his ego. "I won't," I reply sunnily, as if I haven't heard the dark note in his tone. "But you heard the King - he had nothing but compliments for you. Practically offered you the Royal Theatrical Troupe position based solely on the sweep of your hat!"

He gives me a sharp look, and I can see him, oscillating between distrust and and the temptation to delight in me stroking his ego. He gives in, grin broad. "I reckon we're in with a chance," he says, and then I'm forced to move my feet as he sits on the end of the chaise, one casual hand curling around my calf.

It's all I can do to keep the cheerful expression on my face and not yank my leg away.

I hate having to play this game. But at least I'm good at it. I'd want to be, the years I've spent perfecting it.

And right now, I need to be able to show off my beauty and my range to the whole court. Elouise has generously laid the path for me to walk with her mention of me in the recommendation. I just need to fulfill their expectations and then find a way to put the second letter in front of the king.

And that all starts with Killeen.

"We don't have long to prepare," Melia says softly, pouring herself a glass of fruit juice from a tall glass carafe.

"They have dragonfruit!" Delina exclaims. "I haven't seen these since we did that tour around Ascelin. You know, the one where we lost Emeril."

Joseph sends her a look. "Melia's right. What are we going to perform?"

"Nothing too naughty," Pearlene observes slowly. "Or the Queen will be in the King's ear."

"We want to confirm the story Elouise told about us," I say, as if the thought is just occurring to me. "I wonder about The Lament of Caarin? Or is that too sad?" It's definitely too sad but if I propose anything directly, Delina won't be able to help herself - she'll automatically speak against it.

"What about The Last Quinkas?" Stemen proposes.

"Too martial. It'll appeal to the men but the women will be bored by interval."

Joseph's dark eyes are unreadable as they rest on me. "Perhaps The Rose of Delphi?" He names the play I'd considered the best option for me. I give him a small smile.

Silence falls as they all consider it. Finally, Pearlene says, "It's perfect. If we're not too rusty?"

"Liv's never rusty, are you, lass?" Killeen's voice has a thrumming note in it, and his hand is sliding up to my knee.

I leap to my feet. “Rusty or no, I’d better go over a few scenes with Stemen and Delina,” I say quickly, offering him a glowing smile to make up for putting myself out of reach of his hands. “I’m sure the guard will show us where we can rehearse!” I make a show of glancing from face to face. “That is, if that’s the choice?”

“Both of you girls will get a good showing in it,” Pearlene says agreeably.

“It’s the best choice,” Killeen says hurriedly. He rises. “But I’ll come and help smooth out the lumps.”

My heart sinks but I give him another brilliant smile. Focusing on my playing while having to manage Killeen getting handsy sounds a lot like hard work. “Excellent!”

The dressing room we are shown to just before sunset is just as sumptuous as our suite, but better lit. I’ve carried my bag full of cosmetics from my room, but when we arrive, there are a series of maids who offer curtsies and assistance with our makeup.

My eyes widen at the sight of their collection: powders in every hue, small pots of inky black, an array of smooth beeswax-scented pinks and corals and reds, and clean new brushes in every size.. . Melia gives me delighted grin and I’m not even playing as I return it.

“My girls are exceptional,” says a tall, slender woman with golden skin and slender amber-flecked eyes. “You won’t need any of your own powders.”

She sounds dismissive, so I smile at her winningly. “Do you manage this collection? You must be ready for whoever it is that walks through that door!”

My enthusiasm thaws her a little, and my minor manipulation works: all of her girls might be good, but my attendant has a painter’s artistry in her fingertips. Before she’s done, I’m staring at the glass, imagining what it would be like to kiss my own plump red lips, whether in my character's boyish disguise or her dramatic unveiling. Her quick gaze is almost like a bird's, and she's serious until she's completed the final touch: applying a slick lacquer that makes my lips glossy. Then she gives me a satisfied smile in the glass, and I grin back.

"You are extraordinary," I murmur, reaching for her hand. "Thank you. So much. It's nerve-wracking, playing for the court, and this character has to walk the line of being handsome and beautiful. But now I won't have to even think about how I look." I hesitate, looking at her dark eyes in the mirror. "What is your name? I would like to ask for you again, if I may?"

"Alsyn," she whispers nervously. "And if you think I have done well, would you mention it to Mistress Carfellian? She... thinks I fuss."

"I think I've never looked better," I say softly. "And I will tell her so."

As it turns out, I barely have the opportunity for more than that before Killeen comes rushing in the door. "Are you ready?" He asks, breathlessly excited. "Because it's ten minutes to curtain."

My heart leaps sideways in my chest, beating fast, and I automatically take a deep slow breath to try and calm myself. "I just need my boots on," I reply.

Killeen's eyes roam hungrily over my face and down across my chest, despite the mannish shirt. I can feel my face wanting to draw into a fierce scowl, but instead I just regard him coolly. He doesn't notice for a long minute, and then clears his throat, having the minor grace to look slightly guilty.

The sooner I'm shot of him the better.

We each take it in turns to peek out beyond the wings at the audience arrayed before the stage. My mouth falls open at the extraordinary dresses and head-dresses the women are wearing: tight corsets and wide hoop skirts with colorful embroidered fabric draped over them, and hats that seem designed to draw attention away from the wearer, with an array of flowers, decorated with butterflies and insects that I realize after a moment are made of silk. It's like watching a cheerful rabble of parrots and parakeets squawking over a banksia full of seeds.

"Isn't it gorgeous? Seeing them all like this?" Melia is crouched below me, peering out as well. "They're all so beautiful." She sighs. "I wish I could have a dress like that."

"Even my fanciest costume is nothing to these," I reply in a low voice. "Imagine a ball with this lot!"

Stemen hisses at us to get into position, and we scramble to find the right wing to wait behind. I repeat the key cues to myself in my head, checking that my dark curls are firmly tucked up into my ludicrously feathered hat.

This play has always been one of my favorites, but it was Des's as well, and it means I have such mixed emotions about it that I often avoid playing it if I can. But it was unavoidable today.

It's the play that drew Des to me. We'd performed on a rough, uncovered stage at the edge of the common, and afterward she'd approached me, tongue-tied and with her heart in her eyes. She'd been a sweet little ragamuffin of a village innocent, all open hearted and vulnerable - everything I knew had been stolen from me by my harsh childhood.

But being with her had lent me some of that wonder and I'd been hungry for it. Picton had given in and let her join the troupe and for a few months, we'd been so ludicrously enamored that the rest of the troupe took to rolling eyes over me - and for the first time I could remember, even this mild teasing hadn't bothered me.

But my past couldn't be wiped out, not even by the flame-like intensity of her adoration.

It had started as feeling like I didn't deserve what she offered me - that it couldn't be true. Or that there were limits she wasn't prepared to own, however much she vowed there weren't. And then I'd found myself testing the boundaries, certain that there would be some part of me that she couldn't accept. Some of this was sincere: I'd learned that I wasn't ever prepared to have my freedom

- whatever that might mean - circumscribed by another, especially where my desires were concerned. Monogamy wasn't going to ever be for me, and I knew that might lead to rejection.

But some of my testing wasn't of real needs; and even where it was, I didn't gentle the impact or help Des work out whether she could live with it. I pretended everything I did was reasonable; every time I slept with someone else, every time I turned away from her; that if she was hurt, it was just a sign she didn't love me enough, or that some fundamental incompatibility lay between us.

But I was too young and foolish to see that driving someone away by doing something I didn't truly want to do wasn't going to reveal the truth of her love.

It just revealed how deeply fucked up I was.

And even so, she stayed, far beyond what anyone should have done. And then guilt ate me up, and I told myself that she expected too much; that she was making me guilty about who I truly was. I couldn't touch her anymore; nor be touched by her. The guilt and unwarranted anger and disgust at myself combined to make her love unbearable, and I too became unbearable, even to myself. I told myself it must be her who made me so.

Probably the opposite was true. Her love was a mirror in which I could see the monster I'd been made into and I smashed that mirror into shards.

She'd left, finally. And I'd pretended it meant nothing with a ferocity that might have killed me.

I had to change troupes. I left Picton and joined Killeen.

I swallow, banishing Des's face from my mind. This is the last thing I need to be contemplating. Especially right before I have to play. I pinch the skin of my inner arm, hard. The pain is clarifying.

The curtains draw back.

Killeen takes to the stage, his voice rumbling and resonant - clearly the acoustics in this hall are second to none - and then I am wandering onto the stage, performing at being a woman playing at being a man, lost and alone and charming.

But as the moment of climax arrives and I sweep that ridiculous hat from my head to reveal the cascade of curls - the audience gasping and laughing in delight - my mind is filled with the memory of the wonder that infused Des's upturned face that night.

I deserve every last agony I ever inflicted on her, ten times over.

But guilt is useless.

She's gone.

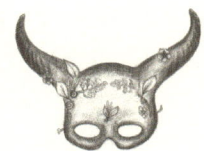

The Convenor congratulates us as we emerge in a laughing, raucous pile from backstage, the heady affirmation of the applause still ringing in our ears. There's nothing like playing.

The Convenor wears a smile that feels like a prize. "Congratulations! What a performance. They will be talking of it for the rest of the season. The King has already had me ensure you will perform again two days hence. And in the meantime, he has invited all of you to the celebration they are holding tonight."

"Celebration? What are they celebrating?"

The Convenor looks at Melia with faintly raised brows. "Nothing in particular. Being royal, perhaps?"

I laugh. "I could help celebrate that, I reckon!" I loop my arm through Joseph's. "But I fear we have nothing as gorgeous as any of those gowns out there."

"We have not had time to arrange a fitting for you all," the Convenor replies, with clear regret. "Tomorrow we will do so, for the night of your second performance. For tonight, I will open the costuming wardrobes for the Royal Theater so that you might present well."

I give them a sidelong look. "This seems very generous. Do all troupes receive such access?"

They raise a single brow at me. "Am I not a gift horse, Mistress Equitor?"

I laugh again, letting the sound ring in the hallway. "Forgive me," I reply. "And might we have access to these wardrobes to perform in, two days hence?"

"That would unfortunately look like favoritism to the other candidates," they say regretfully. "But I may be able to sneak some costume jewellery out. If the Keeper of the Wardrobe looks the other way. This way, please."

The headiness of the performance is still filling my chest and I giggle like a schoolgirl at the prospect of wearing fancy royal costume jewellery. Joseph and I skip together along the hallway ahead of the group, dancing in laughing circles whenever we take a wrong turn.

The Convenor holds open a door to the crowd of us and we tumble through it, but as I pass them, they grab my arm. "We share a dear friend," they tell me, dark gaze fixed on mine. "She bade me help you with your... plans. I am arranging some people for you to meet - those who can help you with the business side. But you must get the Royal sign off. This week, you are flavor of the month. But that will not last. Make the most of your evenings, won't you? The King has agreed that you may attend the festivities tonight and after your second performance. It is a rare honor."

Their words are like cold water thrown over my head. I've been thinking like a player in a troupe, falling back into the same old steps I've always trod. And now here is Elouise, ensuring that I get the encouragement and reminder. I swallow and stiffen my back. "I will work out how to," I say firmly.

They hesitate. "And be careful of the Prince. He is known as a rake."

I give them a grin. "I've handled rakes before."

They give me a speculative look.

And then they nod and step through the door ahead of me. I draw a breath and follow.

CHAPTER TEN

Half an hour later, we are all dressed in more extravagant clothes than we've ever worn. It's not just the silks, though the fabrics are gorgeous enough that I struggle to keep from stroking them repeatedly. The embroidery and needlework is so precise and so subtle as to be practically like paintings brushed over the material.

Even though the fit isn't perfect, since they weren't made for us, we make a good showing. Killeen is practically glowing, he's so delighted. Actually we all are - I love both the look and the feel of this extraordinary dress, green to match my eyes and leaving bare my shoulders above a corset. I can't help thinking that the promise of this moment is extraordinary. Maybe this isn't the moment to be moving on from the troupe.

But then, as the Convenor leads us through the winding hallways of the palace, Killeen puts his hand on the back of my waist possessively. It makes a pit open in the bottom of my gut as I hurry ahead to get out of reach of his touch.

No. Elouise is right. I need a way out, and the fact I'm in the palace attending a ball with the royal family means I have more opportunities right now than I might ever have. I'd be a fool not to take them with both hands.

But these serious thoughts settle as the Convenor opens the door to a large room, aglow with golden light and utterly filled with people.

As a child, I'd seen the silks and jewels in flashes of shielded lamplight, beside Isharin as he stole whatever it was he'd been paid for. I'd imagined what it might be like to be rich enough to wear them. But now, as I gaze about me, I can barely believe this isn't just the dream of the gullible child I had been. It's otherworldly.

Beyond the door is all the sumptuous beauty I'd ever been able to conjure. Women in fluttering dresses with tight-bound stays; men the sober punctuation in the crowd; musicians playing above a dance floor; an an array of comfortable, gold-and-red velvet couches set in clusters around the room. It's extravagant and breathtaking and before I have a chance to fully take it in, the crier is announcing us to the room.

"Please welcome Master Redborne Killeen's troupe of players!" There is generous applause. "Our main characters from this evening's performance, played by Stemen Urrindyer, Delina Cork and of course the incomparable Livinia Equitor!" Each of us steps forward in a swirl of skirts or a grand gesture to offer our courtesy to the room. The broad smile I wear is not a performance - there's something soothing to my soul about this kind of recognition.

Is this what it would be like all the time, if we were the Royal Theatrical Troupe?

A flock of waiters sweep forward to offer us food and drink, and we split into two smaller groups to cluster around the small tables set to facilitate game playing or snacks. It's not ideal for eating a meal, but as ever, I'm starving after the performance. I deliberately wait until Killeen has taken his seat, and then sit in the other group to eat.

Even before our meals arrive, we are visited by courtiers. Lady Geraline of Delphi flutters her eyes at Stemen from behind her fan, much to the consternation of her husband, Lord Topher, though he tries to hide it. Duke Ruskit of Roath holds Delina's hand a moment too long, and his fiancee's smile is a little strained. The court loves its players.

But as our food arrives at our table, a rather more momentous occasion presents itself.

"May I pull up a chair here, Mistress Indella?" the voice inquires from behind me. "I would so appreciate making your acquaintance without my mother peering over my shoulder."

I double-take over the name and turn to find the Crown Prince of Rescalin standing behind me, a cheerful smile on his face, and with a servant behind him, holding a chair. He's handsome - handsomer than I would have thought when we met in the Great Hall with his parents. My heart beats into my throat, and I'm struck by hair so black it's like a raven's wing, falling across grey-blue eyes. He's waiting for my response, so I wave a hand rapidly, hoping I'm not flushing too red. "Of course, your highness, please do."

"I don't want to keep you from eating," he says, with charming ease. "So please, do go ahead. But if I may ask you a few questions, between mouthfuls?"

I smile, and his gaze slips to my mouth. Rake indeed. This is almost a gift; men like this are easy to manipulate, usually. "I'd be delighted, your highness, though I'm not sure what I could know that you do not already have an intimate knowledge of."

Using the word 'intimate,' despite its innocent context, is enough. His eyes darken just a smidge, and inside, I crow. Excellent. If he wants me, hopefully I can get what I want out of him. A way in with his father. Maybe even vouching for me.

"I wouldn't have the first clue what it's like to perform on stage in front of people," he says with a laugh.

"Do you not, your highness? I could have sworn I saw a young man of your description up on a stage earlier today." I offer a playful smile, and he laughs.

"I had never quite thought of it like that!" he replies. "But the dais is quite like the stage. Though there are some differences. I only wish I could stop playing at being the Prince occasionally."

I regard him, falsely solemn. "Are you certain you do not shed your princely character of a night, with your crown?" I gesture to the circlet that rests in his hair. "Do you not feel the weight when a servant takes it off?"

He grins in delight at me. "It's true that it's relief when they put it away," he replies, chuckling, and leaning close, he adds confidingly, "But they still obey my every word, even when I've not a stitch on!"

I laugh at this, sipping at my wine and wondering whether I should take the opening for innuendo that he's so generously given me. The flirtation is fun, and my blood is stirring. And with his gaze sparkling at me, I know that if I didn't have a purpose here at court, I'd not be going to bed alone tonight.

But Elouise's warning resonates in my mind. If I let myself be reduced to a jade in their eyes, I'll never be seen as capable of leading a troupe. "Your servants sound both exceptionally devoted and remarkably tolerant," I tease. "Though perhaps they need more of a theatrical education: even most children know a player is no longer the character when they shed their costume."

Even if there's a shadow of disappointment in his eyes, that I haven't taken up the chance to weave more references to his nudity into the conversation, he chortles nonetheless, and replies, "You look as if you need some more wine, mistress. Shall we see if this tests the limits of my servant's devotion?"

I frown as if in deep thought. "I suspect that their tolerance may be more tested by being required to play at servant to a player in place of a prince. I mean, I don't even have the circlet to make believe!"

Behind him, his manservant gives me a quick grin, an expression that somehow communicates his appreciation for my banter, offers a brisk yet precise bow, and disappears. "See? He wanted to fetch it for you." Shandor smiles in satisfaction.

I raise an arch eyebrow. "Perhaps I am more easily pleased than his usual princely responsibilities?" I want to add, Or perhaps he is merely appreciative that I am not making my demands sans clothing, but it's unwise. I bite my tongue again. After a lifetime of being primed for every playful piece of innuendo, it's surprisingly difficult to keep my lips closed on it, especially knowing that my conversational partner would rather that I did go there.

And it's so clear he would fuck me in a heartbeat. He's monopolizing my time, ignoring the rest of Killeen's crew, calling me Indella after a character I played who also fucked a prince, laughing at my jokes, offering me more wine - nothing like inhibitions being diluted! - and leaning closer to me by the moment.

And gods help me, he's handsome and he's charming and he's a fucking prince.

I can resist him, but it's not going to be fun. I can already feel an irritable little voice in my head speaking back to Elouise's warning. So much hypocrisy. Why shouldn't I just take what I want? A man would never have to make a choice between wanting sex and improving his livelihood. Why should I? Just more evidence of the injustices of this world. I squash the thoughts ruthlessly before they can appear on my face. Practicality. This isn't the moment for railing against injustice. This is the moment for prioritizing the future I want to build for myself.

His manservant returns, weaving through the cluster as Delina and Joseph and Stemen rise and head towards the dance floor with partners. He places a tall glass full of sparkling wine before me with a flourish. I catch his eye and smile. "Thank you," I murmur. I sip at it, watching the dancers trace out their steps.

Then I hesitate a moment, glancing at the Prince and then away - a play, enough to have him leaning in, eyebrow raised quizzically. "I..."

"Yes, mistress? Is there aught else you require? Please, allow me to exercise my princely command and prove my manservant's devotion once more. I'm sure he'd be delighted by the opportunity too."

"Your wish is my command, mistress," his manservant puts in, grinning at me a little too appreciatively. His master gives him a sharp look, and his expression settles back to opaque neutrality.

"This is a Prince's gift I have to beg," I tell him, turning to Prince Shandor again. "I... I need to speak to the King. In private, if possible."

"In private?" Shandor's eyebrows shoot up. "My father? Whatever for?"

I hesitate again, looking away, feigning bashfulness but really scanning for eavesdroppers who would probably be the measure of what I could disclose. Unfortunately Melia is lingering in the table next to ours, and she's looking unduly focused for someone sitting and sipping her wine. "I... I wanted to thank him for his generosity, and ask whether he had a request for our next performance." I give Shandor a smile. "After all, it will be his decision, about the Royal Theatrical Troupe, will it not?"

Shandor makes a faux-disapproving moue of his mouth. "Well, he will of course consult with the family." He leans closer again, his shirt brushing my bare upper arm. I can feel the warmth of his body behind it. "And he respects my opinion deeply when it comes to theater," he murmurs softly, his breath shifting a loose curl against my neck. His gaze is on it, I can tell. Desire is crawling through me, and I have to force my breath to be even.

"I do hope that we will have your vote, your highness," I say, louder than he had spoken, to break the intimacy of the moment. I take a sip of my drink as well, turning my head gently away from him - knowing it highlights the long line of my neck, curving down into shoulder. Gods. This feels like fishing - as I've seen it in some of the villages around Delphi. Playing out enough line, tugging enough to keep the hook in. Somehow I'm not sure this fish is going to weary easily.

"Well, that will depend on your next performance," he says, archly challenging, sipping at his own wine and reclining back away from me into his chair. "Although the taste you gave us earlier today suggested it would be deeply moving. It's a shame my mother is not of the same mind. I was quite touched by the idea of such a beautiful young woman sacrificing herself for her prince. Devotion, tolerance and obedience. What more could any man want?"

I lick my lips, my mouth suddenly dry. He's using every opportunity to push, and now he knows what I want. Or he thinks he does. "I am sure whatever we choose, you will find it... a minor revelation," I say, making myself smile. "But truly, your highness, I would be so grateful for just five minutes of your father's time. Do you think you could arrange that?"

He gazes at me thoughtfully, but there's a canniness, almost a cruelty, in his eyes now. He doesn't like that I'm seeking to get past him. "I could." He sips at his wine, silent. Is he going to say it out loud? Make the jade's bargain right here beside the dance floor? I swallow hard. I hate it when the playfulness gets serious like this. If things are going to get ugly, this is usually the precursor. Then he sighs a breath out his nose. "But only if you'll agree to at least three dances with me, Indella." He gives me a sidelong grin, the humor back in his eyes.

Relief is like gratitude, it's so intense. "Well," I say, playfully drawing out the bargaining, tapping my lip with a fingertip. "Perhaps... but only if at least one of them is a waltz."

He laughs and rises, holding a hand out to me. "I'll make them all waltzes, if it pleases you, Indella. Even if I have to tax the musicians with the command."

I grin up at him, sliding my hand into the warmth of his. The desire is simmering in my bones, and I know it'll take almost nothing to send it soaring around my body. Looks like I'm in for a few nights of self-love, at the rate I'm going. Or I'm going to have to find someone safe. Someone who won't see me as a jade. "Oh no, your highness. I always like knowing what a man's favorite dance is. I feel like it tells me so much about him, somehow."

"You're going to learn all my secrets as we dance?" he asks, sliding my hand into the crook of his arm. The warmth and shift of his muscles under his fine shirt heats my blood further. I leash the desire sharply. I need to play. Keep him on the line. Not pull him in.

"Perhaps," I say, laughing, my dark curls brushing against the bare skin of my shoulders. "Though they can't be much like secrets if I could learn them on the dance floor! I suspect I'd learn more of your secrets from your manservant, if I really wanted to learn them."

"You may not dance with Ruendon," he tells me, mock-severely, "or you might learn all the secrets of Rescalin!"

And as I laugh once more, he spins me out onto the dance floor, tugging me briskly against the warmth of his body. I gasp a little at the small collision and his eyes darken again.

Gods. Fuck.

It's not like fishing. It's like walking a fucking tightrope.

CHAPTER ELEVEN

I wake the next morning after the sun has already risen, feeling slightly sodden.

But I'm waking alone, and in my own bed, which at least means I've kept the Prince on the line but without falling foul of the risk Elouise had hated elaborating on for me.

A small win. But I haven't gotten my moment with the King yet.

I groan as I haul myself out of bed, wrapping myself briskly in a satiny dressing gown and shoving my feet into the zori by the door. To my relief, breakfast has been laid out in the common lounge of our suite. Joseph is bent over a letter at a desk set against the wall. I raise a hand in silent greeting, and he smiles sleepily, reminding me of a cat stretching in sunlight.

I collect a light beginning to a breakfast: chunks of cut fruit - dragonfruit and mango from further north, native plum and peaches, carefully tended in the south - a croissant, and a cup of mate, only slightly over-brewed - and then I wander out the open double doors and down the wide pale stair down onto the soft grass of the gardens.

I could get used to living like this. Breakfast waiting for me. Costumes more stunning than I've ever seen. Clothing made for us on someone else's coin. Living in the palace. Despite the fatigue from last night, I find myself smiling as I cross garden, sticking to the shadows cast by enormous peppercorn and willow trees

The grass is luxurious and after a few steps, I realize I can kick off my zori without fear of thorns or prickles. What kind of luxury is this, to have gardeners literally pull prickly weeds from a lawn. Half of me is horrified by how casually wealth is displayed here, in the tiniest of inconveniences being addressed in advance - while I know there's dozens of girls just like I was, withering on the street before they're even fully grown - and half of me simply revels in it.

Gods know I've earned it.

I sip my mate as I sink onto a carved mahogany bench under a willow and inhale the scent of green deeply.

As I exhale, a small giggle escapes me. This is everything I've dreamed of, and I'm living it. Right now. For just a moment, surely I can just enjoy it.

I rarely feel this kind of intense contentment. In fact, the last time I remember feeling it was either Des, before the limerence faded and my fucked-up-ness reasserted itself. It feels like victory, almost. I'm high enough here that I could spit on Isharin. If he's even still alive.

The bitter thought can't linger in the sunshine, and the croissant is crisp and falls to pieces in my fingers. I lick them clean, and then stare at the dancing pink blooms while I try to think about my next step.

The Prince is my best route to the King. He's reluctant, it would seem, but we did have a deal, however foolish. The question is whether he'll follow through. And whether, in the meantime, his demands might increase.

I purse my lips, wondering. Do I send him a note? Reveal my desperation? Do I remain silent and risk him forgetting me, replaced by gods only know what other beautiful player is here for the Royal Theatrical Troupe selection? Do I tell him why I'm seeking his father's approval? Share with him Elouise's letter? I sigh. Doing so would likely reveal the situation with Killeen - after all, what player would leave her troupe when there's a chance of working in the palace? He can't know how much I need to move on. That's the biggest vulnerability I can see.

The thoughts chase each other around in my mind until I groan aloud and give up, heading back indoors.

Inside, the Convenor is waiting. "They weren't sure where you were," they say, voice that same strong, even tone. Like they're never shaken, or uncertain, or moved. "I'm afraid they've gone without you."

"Gone?" I inquire, setting my soiled crockery on the sideboard.

"Into the city. I thought we might make use of the opportunity. I have someone for you to meet, if you're willing."

I raise my brows. "Someone?"

"He's worked for a troupe before, but he fell during a tumbling performance and his foot had to be amputated. But he managed their tours and their money, before his injury. His troupe leader was drunken fool, but the troupe nonetheless was well known. They even were the Royal Theatrical Troupe, for a season." They give me an even look. "Whatever you decide, you should meet him."

I nod. Elouise's gift, after all. "Very well. But I need a wash."

"You'll pass with him. And then I'll show you the best baths in the palace." They offer a rare smile, and it ignites their countenance and nearly steals my breath.

There's nothing like this kind of switch about - the serious and sober shifting into sunshine - to make me curious. Exactly how do they know Elouise? And well enough to be entrusted with this? Elouise wouldn't put my future in just anyone's hands.

They smile, again, a dimple appearing in their cheek - a sign that they're waiting for a response. How much of my musings has been scribed on my face?

"Let me get dressed," I say, hesitating a moment longer. They know the royal family, surely. Maybe they're the best person to test my strategies with, however much it goes against the grain to trust another so swiftly. Elouise's vouchsafe counts for a lot.

"Of course," they say, prompting me with raised, amused eyebrows.

I hesitate a moment longer and they pin their lips together against laughter before I turn to change.

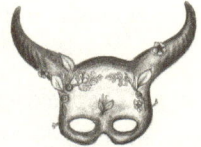

Elouise knows her way around business, and so does the Convenor. And nowhere is it more clear than in their plans for my troupe - my troupe! - gods. Within bare minutes, it is patently obvious that I could cheerfully hand over all the business aspects of running a troupe to Master Precin Carronbout without a second thought.

He's attentive, he listens well as I share uncertainties, corrects misapprehensions generously but with pinpoint accuracy… It's clear that he knows his business inside and out.

And he had seen our play the night before.

It's difficult to trust someone who can remain unmoved by art, I've found. The detachment required has only ever been associated with a capacity for cruelty in my life. But even the memory of our performance has him pressing a hand to his chest, lost for words.

His blue eyes, sunk into wrinkles of pale skin, glisten. "I have so missed being on the road with a troupe," he says, in a voice that has shifted from the fastidious precision he used when discussing the practicalities of finance and banking. It's resonant, warm, vibrating with feeling. "I have missed seeing such audacious, aspirational performances such as you gave us all last night." He reaches out a hand to clasp mine, his gaze on mine so sincere it makes my eyes water. "You are exceptionally talented, mistress. It would be an honor to watch you put together a troupe of your own."

"You are too kind, Master Carronbout," I reply, with the tone that makes light of a compliment.

"Truly, mistress. I miss the art of it. I would take half pay for the first year, would you have me." I must have blinked at him in shock, because he adds, "I am an old man. I do not have family. I have already given my life and my limbs -"

he gives a faint smile at the hard joke, "- and now, I just want more art to sustain me. Above all things."

There's something bemusing and gratifying about this old man's sincere love of playing. So I wrap my hand over his, thank him for his time and for giving me much to think on, and promise to be in touch. He deflates a little, but rises and offers a gracious bow. At the door, he pauses and turns to add, "I know that being part of the Royal Theatrical Troupe would count for much, mistress... But I do not think it would take many years for a troupe with the two of us within it to reach that zenith ourselves." His piercing blue gaze slices into me. "In case you wondered."

And then he's gone.

"Well," I say into the silence. The Convenor raises a brow but doesn't say anything. I clear my throat thoughtfully. "What exactly is the Duchess to you, that you would help me like this?"

The Convenor just smiles a small secret smile and doesn't reply. "Would you like to see the baths, as I promised?"

I narrow my eyes at them, and then shrug. "I will not be shocked or jealous if you tell me you are lovers," I venture. Nothing like a mystery to draw me in. I regret saying anything almost immediately.

They laugh, a warm sound that nonetheless makes me flush. "I was dandled on her knee as a child. She and my mother... well, they were... close. And when I refused to play at being the man my father thought me, and he forced me to step aside from the family name and title... well, my mother sought her assistance." Rescalin might have a Rover legacy, with space for those who refused to be contained by a sex and where couples of the same sex were welcome. But that legacy has been overwritten by many other less open values. It seems the Convenor's father took his cues from the latter.

"She helped me into this position, before she left court. It was a greater gift than I can ever repay, truly." They give me a sidelong look. "You are a curious one, aren't you?"

I raise a shoulder. "Maybe."

They give me a measuring look, neither friendly nor unfriendly, just scrutinizing. "I am not averse to sex," they say after a long pause. "If that is what lies behind this curiosity of yours. I prefer women to men, when it comes down to it. You need only ask. I am an open book, though many tell me my countenance is intimidating." They rise from the table, their words hanging in the air, demanding a response. "The baths?"

I gaze up at them, pondering. The bluntness is odd. Half the fun lies in the play, in the ambivalence and the uncertainty. Usually the chase is where my appetite is sharpened. But they are beautiful in their own way, and somehow I am curious. "The baths," I agree, and the corner of their mouth quirks that I entirely avoid responding to the rest of what they've said.

But as they lead me down a long flight of stairs, the walls turning to stone and opening out into a cave as the air grows heavier, I watch the gentle twitch of their slender hips and wonder how this straightforwardness might manifest if I touched them. Their trailing fingers on the rough carved banister are long and strong and I find myself wondering what it would be like to have them reaching inside me.

It's not new, these kinds of wonderings - they're familiar as my own breath. And as they lead me through steam wreathed caverns, I swiftly sort the risks, weighing them.

As if I could ever tolerate my desires being constrained.

They slip through a narrow doorway that looks like it might lead into a storage cupboard, but instead a narrow corridor curls away from the main thoroughfare and into a small green room. Not painted green, but festooned with leafy growth and thick moss surrounding a wide still pool. Light steam curls over the surface.

When they pause and turn to me, I smile slow and playful and they hesitate a moment, pupils dilating and then I find myself grinning. I hadn't expected it to be that easy.

"Has anyone ever mentioned that grinning like you've won a fight at the first sign of desire tends to douse the fire before it's even caught?" they ask dryly, but I can hear the edge behind the words. I know that edge in myself - the edge honed on hurt - and I've spent a lifetime working out how to hide it far away.

There's a thread of me that has only seen these moments of revealed underbelly in others as a target. Gods know I'd not been able to still my hand against Des's gentleness back then. But I've learned something through that loss, and now just knowing where the scars lie is sufficient to settle the fierce, cornered dog that lives within me. Knowing I can hurt if they come at me is enough. I no longer need to hurt them before they hurt me. Mostly.

I gaze at them solemnly. "Is it truly doused?" I step towards them, and their hands rise. Are they seeking distance or proximity? I stop. "Would you let me see how thoroughly?" I ask in a breathy whisper.

Their pupils dilate again. "Gods, what even are you?" they ask eventually. "She warned me you tended to act on any desire that came in range but..."

"She said that?" I chuckle delightedly.

"I don't think she meant it as a compliment," they say, almost cuttingly, then hesitate, clearly regretting it.

I laugh even louder at that. "Oh I know she did," I reply softly. "And now you've led me to this gorgeous, secluded bath, and only you and I are here." I tilt my head, taking a slow step toward them, raising my hand to curl against their chest. There's a leather pouch beneath their shirt, and I wonder momentarily what treasures it holds. "So if this is indeed not what you want, you likely need to express that." Their breath shudders into their lungs and I can feel the heart beating below my fingertips speed up. "I want nothing that you don't want, but you should know there's a long list of ways I'm hearing you ask me to fuck you..."

It's delightful, watching this person who has struck me as cool and precise and proper struggle to find the words.

"You'll risk it all, if anyone finds out," they finally say in a low voice. "But it kills me to even say this aloud, frankly."

"Are you going to go off and tell the Prince how I perform in bed?" I ask archly. "Or perhaps take the Queen aside and - "

"Gods, stop," they say in an irritated rush. "Shut up and kiss me."

And I grin - true triumph this time - and tangle my fingers in the gold silk of their shirt and kiss them deep and thorough. When we part, they're breathless and their eyes are dark pools in their face. My fingers are moving rapidly over their buttons, the silk falling open to reveal warm brown skin. Their hands are sliding my skirts up and their hands against my thighs are unbearably hot. "Alright, Mistress Equitor." Their tone is back to the precision with which they had enunciated everything before we entered this cave complex, belied only by being out of breath. "Tell me what you like, because you're going to have to come first."

"If you insist," I murmur. "But it seems a little early to be talking of coming when we're not even naked yet."

"Very well," they offer one of those rare smiles. "Let us prioritize ridding ourselves of our clothes."

The afternoon is a slow, heady unfolding of pleasure, and I find myself wondering halfway through if I've ever known someone with skin as sensitive as the Convenor's. They shiver and shudder the gentler my fingertips become. It's a far cry from the bold, rough handling that so many seek out, and it takes me a moment to attune. The heady gasps they give when I do make it worth it.

But the pleasure is intertwined with political ponderings.

We rest in the heated water, my head drowsing against their shoulder, and the curls around my face becoming perfect corkscrews in the damp heat. My cunt is throbbing, another orgasm slowly fading as my breathing settles as well. "The King is distracted," the Convenor is saying slowly. "He has many grand political concerns. Perhaps it is better to lean into Prince Shandor's attentions. See if that will give you a way to the King."

I splash lazily at the water. “You think he’d vouch for me? Would the King act on his recommendation?”

“It’s not like he hasn’t seen you perform. And he signs off on at least a dozen new troupes every year. Few of them make it, of course, and none to date have been led by women, but then, few of them have Master Carronbout to support them.”

I sigh. “The Prince... it’s already clear. He’s interested in me. But more in fucking me than in helping me, probably.” I splash water so that it flies up, the droplets creating a dark pattern as they hit the stone wall. “It’s going to be hard to keep him on the hook but not drawn in.”

The Convenor purses their lips in a way that just makes me want to kiss them again. “Perhaps it’s the performance then? But you only have one more opportunity... the masquerade afterward is perhaps an opportunity.”

“And Killeen will decide what we will perform.” I wrinkle my nose. “And it would seem that the Prince enjoyed our original performance over much. He called me Indella. The character’s name from The Player and the Prince. Even after seeing me play at being a man last night.”

The Convenor shakes their head. “Men.” They roll their eyes. “Noble men especially. They behave like everything is designed for their entertainment.”

“Don’t I know it?” I sigh. “Well, not much for it. I think I’ll need to ask him directly, sooner rather than later. If he’s not my way to the King...”

The Convenor nods. “It’s a shame really. The King is a lot less guided by his cock, if you can just get to him.”

“A beneficial characteristic in a king, I’d have thought,” I murmur.

“Perhaps... perhaps there’s a way for me to distract the Prince? Long enough for you to be able to present the letter to the King. You would have to be bold, in your approach, but this will be the last chance.”

I gaze at them a moment, pondering. I don’t like plans that aren’t all mine, but they’re here, and they’re offering. And I cannot both distract Shandor and approach the King at the same time. “You would find a way to distract him?”

"I had considered adding a Rover fortuneteller to the masquerade." They tap their lip thoughtfully, and I grin, resisting the desire to kiss them. A distraction. "If I did, I could ensure I timed it for as you made the approach to the King."

"Oh, that sounds... perfect, except that I don't get to have my fortune told then!"

They give me a serious look. "I'm sure we would find time for you, but..." They glance down at the pouch still resting on their chest, damp fingers closing . "I would also happily read for you, should you wish it. Once we emerge from these baths." They raise fingers gone wrinkly with too much water.

I tilt my head contemplatively. "I would like that. But I like your plan too, for the Prince. It will be enough, I think." I shift, straddling them swiftly. "It's a tightrope either way. But right now, if I have to live for the future when I walk out of here, then let me sink into this present."

They tilt their head, gazing at me silently for a long moment. "I wish I could do more to help. But I will do what I can."

The corner of my mouth curves up. "So tell me what you want in exchange, then, go on," I invite playfully.

They stiffen. "I don't do this as a transaction," they say in a low, intense voice.

"Nor do I," I say, my voice harder than I intend. "But occasionally I play at it." I flutter my eyelashes. "Oh, Convenor, make me your jade," I say melodramatically, pressing a hand against my chest like a poor player in a two-bit tavern.

They roll their eyes again. "Alright, alright."

They're not quite jollied out of their fit of solemnity, but I grin and slide a gentle fingertip down across the sensitive skin of their neck to their chest, barely touching them. I watch as the fine hairs stand on end, and their breath comes short, then smile again. "If you don't tell me what you want, I'm liable to do this for the rest of the evening and leave you desperate."

They look at me from under heavy lids. "So long as I get to make you come again... that sounds like utter bliss."

I blink at them slowly, biting my lip and then grinding my cunt against where they are slowly hardening yet again. "You want me to leave you wanting?"

They smile so slowly it makes my spine tingle with the promise that's heavy in it. "I love carrying the density of arousal around with me. Like a secret. No one knows but me, and all they see is the upright, severe Convenor." They lick their lips and I find myself watching their tongue. "It's like my own kind of play." Their long fingers slide across my hips and graze against my swollen clit, making my own breath shudder out.

"As you wish," I murmur, and press towards their touch.

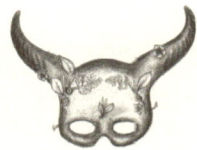

When we emerge from the water, my skin prickling into goosebumps in the cooler air, I feel languorous and slow, like the slow pleasure has sapped my strength. The Convenor perches on the edge of a narrow stone bench, a towel wrapped around their hips. I tighten my own towel as they open the leather pouch around their neck and smile up at me. The cards are not made of paper, but of some kind of very thin wood, gently warped, browned with the contact of old fingers. Both sides are decorated with images made of slender scorch lines. They're old, clearly, and my fingers twitch. I want to reach out and touch them.

"I am new to this, but this deck is not. The cards came from a Rover, old and wise. She died, and left these as a gift for me. It was... it is for her that I am learning to read."

I tilt my chin. "How long have you been learning?"

They hesitate. "It's not like... not like learning to read or to add sums. It's different. It's about learning to understand what they're saying. Like getting to know someone. Slow, mostly, and even when you think you know them backwards, there will be some new corner to discover."

I smile, intrigued, and sit beside them, watching their long fingers gently shuffling the cards, their gaze on me. "So how does this work?"

"I know only the simplest of strategies, but it works, usually." They straighten the deck and hand it to me. "You shuffle, as much or as little as you want to. Then you put your hand over it, and ask a question, then draw a card. And it will be some part of the answer to your question."

I swallow, unexpectedly unsteady, and meet their calm dark gaze. I take the deck, shuffling gently, mindful of the age and provenance of them. "Enough?"

"That is up to you, Livinia," they reply, and somehow their profound calm makes me feel even more restless. Like I'm cozying up to something I don't fully understand.

"Enough," I say, shoving my uneasiness away. I've never believed in fate; if I had, no doubt I'd have given up after the fourth time I got knocked back into the gutter. Or when Des left me. Or... I dismiss the thoughts. Future. Not past. Future. "Now I ask the question?"

They hold out their hand, the little pile of cards in the center of it. I cover the deck with my hand, and somehow the long path I've taken to the palace flashes through my mind. My heartbeat kicks up. "What does the future have in store for me?"

The Convenor's dark eyes glimmer at me as they fan the cards out gently. "Choose your card, Livinia," they murmur softly, invitingly.

I draw a slow breath, reaching out to take a card. As I pull it free, gripping it firmly, another falls free. I look at the card I'm holding and blink at it. The Lovers, it says, and depicted on the face of it is one person gripping at the face of another, bending them to their kiss. I stare at it, blinking, desperately trying not to find Des's face in the picture and failing. My self-control falls apart, my mind suddenly flitting after her - an image of her laughing, of her weeping, of her mouth soft with pleasure.

No. Surely not. She's gone. I fucked that one good and proper, and there's no way. No way. Surely no way.

My heartbeat beats into my throat, and I swallow hard, clutching at the threads of my capacity to play. It doesn't have to be Des. It couldn't be, but maybe it could mean someone else? Could it?

I glance up at the Convenor. Their lips are slightly parted, and they're staring at the card that fell to the ground. It's face up, and reads 'The Traitor,' and depicts someone who looks both terrified and angry. I feel heat flush over my skin. "Does..." My voice dies, and I clear my throat. "What does that mean?"

"I..." The Convenor clears their own throat, and for once they sound awkward. "You drew the Lovers. There is love in your future."

I raise incredulous eyebrows, tossing The Lovers card back onto the pile in their hand. "Oh, like it's that simple, right?" I say, and I'm conscious my voice is hard, almost indignant. Betraying myself. Dread unfurls in my gut. I snort softly. "And The Traitor is meant to signify nothing?"

The Convenor looks at me steadily, then raises a shoulder. "Perhaps. It can also signify betraying one's own desires, or... perhaps one's own ethics."

I huff out a breath, irritable at the spell the possibility of a future has cast over me. "Looks like more of the same, then." My voice is still hard, even though I know I need the Convenor's goodwill. "Or maybe this is just telling me about my past. Never known a love I couldn't find a way to fuck up." The bitterness is palpable, almost honest. I bite my tongue - literally bite it to keep more words from falling from my lips. Dread unfurls in my gut; they must not see. Time to get out before I give myself away.

"Did you think of the past when you asked your question?"

"Oh perhaps. Probably. Or it's just a fucking card." It's a couple of pieces of wood. I'm a fool for even thinking it could mean anything. I want to be gone now, away from their steady gaze.

I rise, rapidly loosening the towel and grabbing at my dress to haul over my head, and shoving my still-damp feet into my shoes. "Thank you for a magical afternoon," I murmur, injecting as much softness into my voice as I can, aware that the contrast with what's come before is likely to put the lie to it. I bend to kiss their cheek, and as I do, the card yet lying on the floor stares up at me.

Without looking back, I stride out of the clammy humidity of the room, long strides carrying me away.

CHAPTER TWELVE

The Slayer of Pastira is a play of high stakes and drama, and when we take to the stage once more a few days later, I play a Princess readying herself to flee ahead of a dragon attack. The histories tell us that this is based on real events, but I always wonder. Could dragons really disappear so completely from the world, after devastating it so entirely? Without any real explanation?

My role in the story is to sell the threat - a threat it's impossible for us to depict directly on the stage without significant costuming. And so I pitch my voice high, and spend much of the play clutching at the arms of knights (Stemen), my father the King (Killeen), and my lady in waiting (Melia).

"Please, father, do not send me away!"

"The dragons are coming, my child." Killeen strokes fingers down my face. I steel against reacting. "You must be safe, in case I am not. You will be our people's only hope for the future."

"But I am afraid," I wail. "I cannot sleep for fear they will attack while we are vulnerable."

"Your highness, be assured, we set a watch in the towers. We will not be caught unawares," Stemen puts in, with a brisk bow. "But you must heed his majesty, your highness. You must flee. We cannot lose all of the royal family at once!"

I clutch my hands together, twisting them. "Very well," I say, my voice shaking. "If you will promise that you will keep my father safe."

"I swear it on my life," Stemen says, falling to one knee. "But will you give me your favor before you leave?"

There's a resonant "oh!" from the audience that makes my heart swell. There is nothing as satisfying as having a whole crowd of people hanging on your every word.

I let my breath catch in my throat, as if on a sob. "It is the very least I can do to show my regard and my trust in you, Sir Timble."

I reach out a hand to Melia, who presses a scarf into it, which I wrap around Stemen's upper arm. "May you stay safe, my hero," I stage-whisper, with a sideways glance at Killeen. "I will be exceptionally displeased if you were to go and do something as foolish as dying."

An appreciative chuckle rumbles through the watching audience.

That marks the end of act 2, and the beginning of the end. I exit the stage with Melia, and tug the circlet from my hair. A scarf tied over my hair and a shawl around my waist and I'm Felda, no-nonsense owner of a Pastira tavern. After Pearlene's narrative introduction, I sweep onto the stage with my fists on my hips. "Not sure why we're paying our taxes when the King just sends his own family to safety while we're left here, ready to be burnt with our livelihoods!"

And so the final act begins. I only have a few key lines in this act, but at the very end, as part of the denouement, I return to the stage as the Princess, with Melia at my side.

"There's nothing left," she says.

"Nothing at all," I reply, my voice trembling. "I cannot imagine how anyone could..."

"You never know," Melia says comfortingly, her arm wrapped around my shoulder. She sends a dubious glance over her shoulder at the audience that makes them giggle in brief commiseration with her.

"No one could survive this," I say, my voice growing stronger. "But we have. Rescalin has." I bend, picking up the favor I'd tied around Stemen's arm earlier.

"It may have been foolish youth that let us love as we did. But it was hope as well. And that hope did not die with the dragons."

The rest of the cast shuffle onto the stage, their faces blackened with charcoal. I turn to them, drawing a deep breath. "My people, know this. We will rebuild this great city, greater than it ever has been. We will rebuild it as a monument not only to the memories of all those we have lost, but to the strength that they have lent us. For it is that strength that will allow us to make our way into the future. A future that no dragon fire could extinguish. A future that will be a testament to the sure truth: Rescalin's star will not be dimmed."

And as the curtains drop into place before us, the applause is deafening. I grin in delight, my heart light, and Melia squeezes my hands, giggling. It's such a heady feeling, the moment of applause. We hurry into our line as the curtain rises to allow us to bow and curtsy, and my heart soars again as I realize they're rising to their feet.

A standing ovation.

I glance sideways. Joseph is stoic as ever, but Stemen's grin is broad and irrepressible. Pearlene looks almost smug and Killeen rolls his mustache, his teeth showing below. Even Delina's face is alight, nothing more than pleasure on it for once.

In this moment, it feels like we are an actual troupe, together.

And the curtains fall again, and the moment evaporates.

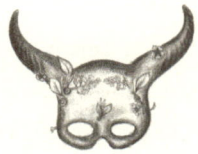

The Convenor leads us back to our suite where there are a half dozen seamstresses and clothing made to fit all of us. They must have taken our measurements last time they were here, and worked the day through to have them ready.

But they're gorgeous.

A seamstress holds mine out for me to look at. A matte, dusky rose color, and the fall of the dress is from my low hips, with the corset emphasizing the dramatic curve from waist to hip. It makes me grin as soon as I see it, and when I turn, delighted, I find the Convenor, smiling one of those rare, pleased smiles. It warms me.

"Will you put it on, Mistress?" The seamstress is anxious. "My master wants to see that it fits. He made me bring a needle and thread, just in case the measurements were off."

The dress feels like heaven against my skin, and the gentle line of the neck, offering just a hint of décolletage but somehow even more evocative for it, is specifically designed, I suspect, to please both the Prince and his mother. When I look in the mirror, my own delighted smile is enough.

It's perfect.

Then Alsyn rapidly makes up my face and holds out a black lace mask, a simple domino but for the fabric. The ribbons are inky velvet and black, green and pink feathers spray from the edge of the lace, like a fan that will sit over the temples. I stare at her. The masquerade. I'd forgotten.

"It's a masquerade tonight. Did they not tell you?"

I take a deep breath to soothe my pounding heart. I adore a masquerade. The not quite being sure who anyone is. The invitation to take people as you find them - whatever that might be - rather than as you expect them to be. She wraps the mask efficiently around my head, and when I gaze in the mirror, I don't even recognize myself.

This is the other thing I love about a masquerade.

It would seem the court thinks similarly of our new garb, and the masks we wear. When we appear, the room falls silent for a split second, then the chatter surges back, louder than before. I glance back at my troupe-mates and smile delightedly. Stemen looks like a pale lion, Melia like a cat, while Joseph's mask is a studded black domino, plain and evocative. Delina is a hawk, the beak curving cruelly over her nose; Pearlene wears a kingfisher's bill and the vibrant blue plumage around her neck, and Killeen wears a mask a handsome fox mask, his hair brushed back.

I glance around swiftly, carefully working out where the Prince is without appearing to recognize him in the corner, playing Royals. He's wearing a tiger mask, orange and black stripes running back into his hair but I can tell it's him by the way he holds his shoulders. The mask shifts my focus to his physique and for a moment I wonder whether this is all too much fuss. Maybe it's just better to give him what he wants.

Then Killeen's orange mask shifts into my peripheral vision and I dip away towards the food. Hopefully the mask will keep the Prince at bay a little, until the Convenor's plan can be executed. It's his father I need to speak with.. "A bite to eat first?" Melia asks in a low voice.

"Can't drink on an empty stomach! That would be unwise." I grin.

We swiftly fill our plates and set about eating. We're half way through the meal when Joseph murmurs, "The Prince is sending his man over."

"Quick! Don't let him catch me yet." I rise quickly, patting my mouth clean and stepping away.

"Playing hard to get?" Delina asks in a cruel tone after me. "With the Prince? Really? I'd have thought you were already on your knees before him."

I curl my lip at her, but don't reply, weaving easily between aristocrats in dramatic doll-like masks, with pursed red lips. They sip at their wine and stare at me. At the door, the Convenor pauses, looking at me from behind a snowy owl mask and white silks. Behind them, a lined brown face surrounded by lightly curled greying hair hovers. I hesitate a moment, and the Convenor gives me a quick nod. It's time.

The crier steps forward to announce the fortuneteller's presence, and I thread my path towards the King. He's bent over a game of orlan with a too-handsome aristocrat. The King wears a green dragon mask, shoved back onto his head impatiently. His companion wears a mask that curves across his cheeks, and it's made of a pure gold - or so it seems.

It's bold, approaching the King directly. But it's possibly my last opportunity.

Behind me, there's loud applause, and then the call for the Prince to have the first fortune told. I dismiss it, glad the King is focussed on the game and seems not to be interested in the Convenor's latest novelty.

He reaches out to move a series of tiles. Something about him makes my gut curdle and I promise myself I'll keep my distance rather than launching straight in. I hesitate, then pause just in his peripheral vision and curtsy deeply, holding the position until he sighs and looks up at me.

"You're the player, aren't you? From tonight's performance? If I don't miss my guess?" The aristocrat's gaze behind the mask rakes over me, and it feels like the premonition of claws.

"I am, my lord. Mistress Equitor."

There's a rush beside me and I turn to find the Prince grinning down at me, his teeth blazing white below the edge of his mask. Fuck. "Ah, my Indella! There you are, I've been looking for you!" I bridle internally at the casual possessive. He offers me his arm, and the scowl begins when I don't immediately take it.

"Your highness!" I exclaim, managing to stay just out of reach. "I am so looking forward to dancing with you in just a moment. But I had a request to make of his majesty your father first if I may, your majesty?" I dip into a curtsy again, keeping my gaze low in the hope he'll take pity on me.

"You're interrupting our game, Mistress Equitor," the cruel aristocrat says sharply.

"Oh enough, Lord Sedjul," the King says wearily, gesturing to me to stand. "What is it, girl?"

My heart pounds hard in my chest but my voice is low and clear thankfully. Many years of practice at keeping calm while panic and terror lap at my heels. "Your majesty, I wish to start my own troupe. I believe I could make a valuable contribution to the artistic life of our great country, if you would offer me your recognition and permission."

I fish under my skirts to find the scroll Elouise had carefully penned all those - gods was it only weeks ago?! "I already have the promise of patronage from the Duchess Elouise. She wrote a letter to you regarding this matter, which I have carefully borne hence."

I pause, with my hand outstretched. The King peers at me but Lord Sedjul speaks first. "Elouise. Pfaugh. She is always trying to pull your strings, even from Scyless. Not part of the court but still wanting the same control she once had." He shakes his head in disdain, and it's all I can do to keep the consternation from showing on my face. I'd had no real sense that this was how Elouise was seen in Pastira. It feels like I've stepped into a puddle and found myself up to my middle in mud. I clutch at my calm and keep my gaze on the king.

"Besides," Lord Sedjul adds. "You hardly have time for this. Not with that northern king coming to negotiate tomorrow. You'll be too busy with matters of state, will you not?"

The King gives me a speculative look and then his eyes fall on his son, the tiger still hovering just behind me. "Give the letter to my son," he says briskly, as if he's pleased to have found a solution. "And I will ask him, in four days' time, whether I should approve your petition." He fixes me once more, his dark gaze pinning me. "Convince him of your plan, and I will approve it."

I hesitate. This seems so risky, my fate being placed directly in the Prince's hands. I smile, and Lord Sedjul skewers me with his sardonic gaze. I hand the scroll to Prince Shandor, unable to suppress the sensation that I'm venturing out over an abyss. "Now, if you might graciously permit us to get back to our game? Mistress Equitor?" Lord Sedjul's expression is almost begging me to misstep.

I mustn't.

"I - yes, of course," I say in a rush. "Many thanks your majesty. I will hope that Prince Shandor's report is convincing. Thank you for your time and apologies for the interruption."

I curtsy, restraining myself from the temptation to bob rudely instead, and then turn, smiling up at Prince Shandor. "I am looking forward to hearing what you would like to see in support of my petition, your highness."

The Prince's wide smile is too wide and my heart sinks. "I will have to think of something good - I mean, to demonstrate your skills, Indella."

I smile at him again, but inside, hope is wilting.

Am I ever going to be able to convince him I'm something other than a momentary fuck?

CHAPTER THIRTEEN

The fortune-teller has barely had a moment to herself all night. The aristocrats have fluttered away to the dance floor, giving those receiving their fortunes a mite more privacy than earlier in the night. Melia returns from her telling serious-eyed and troubled. Delina gives her a speculative look, but when she opens her mouth, Stemen speaks instead. "You should have a turn, Liv. I'd like to hear what your spread looks like."

I know he's just saving Melia from Delina's cruelty, but she turns to me with avid eyes. "Oh yes, let's see what you get, Liv."

"Oh, Indella, yes, let's see what your future holds. Surely more than killing yourself for your Prince!" Shandor drapes fingers against my arm. They're warm and dry, but the use of the character's name makes me want to pull away.

I sigh, remembering The Traitor sitting on the damp floor of the bathing chamber, The Lovers in my hand. My past, surely. Maybe it could be good to hear more about the future. Maybe even some guidance about what to do next with Prince Shandor. I look at him sidelong, and draw a breath. "Alright, yes. But I will do it on my own."

The Prince pouts. "Oh, I want to see!"

I shake my head airily. "My future, my reading, my rules." I rise, and bend until our faces are close enough I can see his pupils dilate. "But if you're very nice to me, I'll tell you all about it."

The Rover woman's round table is behind a wooden screen, only partially hidden from the room. Her deepset eyes meet mine, and I smile winningly. Maybe I can influence this whole thing if she likes me? She regards me seriously. "You wish to hear of your truth, and of your future?"

I draw a deep breath. The Convenor peeps around the screen, meets my eyes briefly and then dips away in a flutter of white silks. "I do."

The deck of cards the Rover woman has are different, the images are colorful compared to the scorched pictures on the Convenor's set. They're made of stiff paper and glimmer in the low light - painted lettering in gold. She hands them to me. "Shuffle, please."

I shuffle the cards obediently, taking my time. My heart is beating in my throat, and I don't want to think about why. I hand the deck back, glancing over my shoulder to make sure none of the troupe have come up behind me. The Rover woman leans towards me and says quietly, "I will lay out eight cards, and then I will explain each of them to you."

I nod, pinching at my wrist gently to keep the dread from unfurling within me. The Convenor's reading was much less thorough. Much more likely to hold accidents of the cards, surely? I don't even know if I believe in this stuff, for fuck's sake.

She lays out the cards into three columns, with two cards to left and right, and four cards in the center. They're all face down, and I stare at them, doubt unfurling within me. I have to fight the urge to shove my chair back.

She hums a little, trailing her fingers over the cards, stroking them almost. She turns over the top card. It's The Hermit, and I glance up at her as her fingers pause on it. "This... is who you were: a hermit, cut off from others; withdrawing in order to find your own voice."

I shiver, just a little. The child I was, withdrawn and alone. Yes, I could see that one. "Alright," I say tersely.

She gives me a mild look. "A question?"

"No," I say, drawing a breath.

"This is how others see you." She turns over the next card, revealing a volcano. I stay silent, staring at the card. "This is destruction, leveling the foundation in order to rebuild better." She gives me a slow look. "Perhaps better? But the devastation must come first." I bite my lips together and nod silently, my hands gripping at each other.

"And this next reveals how you truly are." The next card glimmers in the light as she flips it over, revealing The Moon. She gives me a sharp glance. "It suggests deception, illusion, insecurity, perhaps. A tendency to conceal what you need or want from others, perhaps even from yourself."

They're just cards, I remind myself savagely. It doesn't mean anything. "Oh," I say politely. "I see."

She looks like she's quashing a grin, and I repress the urge to roll my eyes. "And how you would like people to see you." She reveals the next card, bearing the title The River. "As moving forward, with ambition, into fame or renown, being self-assured."

The words are so precise they land like barbs, setting the dread opening in my gut. Too close for comfort. I want to grind my teeth together but I make myself smile as if nothing is wrong. "I see. Aiming for a river and getting a volcano. Anyone would think I didn't play for a living."

She gives me a comfortable smile, not speaking, and I pinch at my own wrist to keep my calm. "And now, we move on to your future - the next three cards outline some of the key turns your life will take," she taps the three next cards. "These are usually roughly in some kind of order. And then we look at who you will be, should you take the path here."

I swallow. This pronouncement makes my skin prickle. But they're just so many cards, just like the Convenor's. Aren't they? I hear a noise behind me, and hold myself steady from turning around.

She turns over the first card.

The Traitor.

It takes everything in me to keep my face smooth at the sight of it. Was it such a happenstance that saw The Traitor emerge with The Lovers, when the Convenor read my fortune days ago?

The fortune-teller's brow rises. "You will betray someone. Or something." The next card is The Gauntlet. "You will… you will endure great suffering. Great suffering, perhaps in sacrifice for some greater good, some end goal you deem to be worth it." I pinch at my wrist, the dread spiraling up. The next card is The Reckoning. I look up at her, suddenly feeling like I need to understand. "Ah yes," she adds softly. "Here it is; if you can face this situation head on, deal with your past, there is a chance for renewal. An opportunity to sort out a complex situation."

"Oh, finally some good news."

She purses her lips disapprovingly at my sarcasm. "You have a complex future. But would you like to see what you will become, at the end of all of this?" The Rover woman looks unimpressed, though whether with the reading or with my reaction to it, I can't quite tell.

"Sure, why not," I reply, shrugging carelessly. "These cards have insulted me at every turn, what more could there be to say?"

She gives me a stern look, and reaches out to flip over the card sitting directly in front of me. At the same moment, the Prince emerges from behind the screen, laughing at someone behind him. "Indella! Come now, tell us all about your spread."

I open my mouth to reply, trying to angle my body to conceal the cards lying on the table, but as I do I glance down at the final card.

The Lovers stares back at me, and my heart shivers within me.

"Ooh. Let's see what you got, Liv!" Delina presses past the Prince, peering over my shoulder. "Oooh, this looks interesting!"

I shove myself to standing, smearing my hand across the cards and messing them from their neat rows. "Oh, it's little more than a trick, Delina. I'm sure they'll say whatever is most flattering for their customers."

The Rover woman snorts. "It can't mean nothing if it's the second time, though, can it? Or perhaps it does. As you will it!" Delina lets out a crow, drawing closer. Is she talking about the Convenor's reading earlier? I frown at her, trying to puzzle it out.

The Rover woman reaches out to collect up the cards before she can see them. "The fates are not to be played with for courtly pleasures." She rises, her brow drawn tight. "Convenor, the fortunes are done being told for the evening. You swore respect, and this..." She swoops her arm at all of us as the Convenor draws closer, their owl mask shoved back. "This is not respect."

"I think we annoyed the Rover." The Prince sounds not remotely concerned about this outcome, and he slides my hand into the corner of his elbow. "Come, Indella. Let us away from this superstition. I will have the musicians play a waltz, and spin you around the floor."

I flirt my way through the rest of the evening with Prince Shandor, having to play stupider than I like to keep from visibly noticing all his double entendre and suggestive hints. We dance, and his cock is hard against my hip. I know it's clear to the entire room that he wants to fuck me. Will they assume I'm sharing his bed that night? I bat back every innuendo and proposal he makes as if we're playing a game of this. Prizes for keeping the ball moving back and forth between us.

It nearly kills me, to have to play at being so obtuse.

But he accepts it, as most men do, and by the end of the evening, I've wrangled from him a promise: I am to direct a performance for him in three days, and this will be the basis on which he will decide my future. When I ask who I should direct, he waves his hand carelessly. "You'll find some performers, I'm sure. After all, aren't you planning to lead a troupe? Surely you must know who you're going to have as part of it?"

I pin my lips together, not trusting myself to respond.

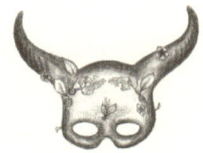

Later, I follow Melia and Joseph as they leave to return to our suite.

"The Rover was... how did you find your reading, Liv?" Melia asks, almost as soon as we leave the room.

"Oh, smoke, mirrors and a side of superstition," I reply, light and careless. I'd rather not examine anything about the spread too closely.

"It probably is, isn't it?" Melia can't let go of the thought.

"No doubt. A distraction for royalty. Nothing more," Joseph says comfortingly.

"It's strange to imagine we're... consorting with royalty...," Melia murmurs as we loop arms, only staggering slightly from the effects of the alcohol. "Prince Shandor seems quite taken with you,"

"He does, doesn't he?" I say with heavy irony. "He might as well shout it from the rooftops."

"Is that what you're waiting for?" Joseph's brows shoot upwards. "I've been wondering what on earth could be keeping you from his bed. You seem to like him well enough."

"I've fucked worse," I say bluntly, grinning when he winces. "But I'm holding out for... well, here's the thing. I need your help."

"Uh oh," Joseph mutters, and Melia looks equally worried.

"I... the Prince wants me to direct a performance. Just for him and his friends. In three days."

"He... wants you to direct?" Melia scowls in confusion. "But why? We already have a director."

Joseph's grey eyes are steady on mine, but the pause is longer than usual. He must have drunk a fair bit tonight. And fair enough. We'd done our final performance. All they're waiting on now is word about the Royal Theatrical Troupe selection. "Are you...?" He shakes his head. "We can't tell Killeen."

I wince. Maybe I should've waited til the next day to talk about this. Joseph was usually more circumspect with risky secrets but clearly he'd drunk enough to drown his discretion. "No," I agree firmly, giving him a severe stare. "We really can't."

He glances swiftly at Melia, who is looking at each of us in turn, bemused. "I don't get it!" She wails finally, also more dramatic than her usual self.

"Shh, let's wait til we're back in our suite," Joseph tells her hurriedly. "But how exciting for us to be performing privately for the Prince!" He's trying to make it up to me by getting Melia on board with the plan. I give him a half hearted smile.

The common lounge of the suite is empty when we make our way inside, Melia fumbling the key. We settle into our chairs, and I'm bleary and tired but also somehow shot through with excitement. I may not sleep before we perform.

"The Prince has invited me to give a performance. He wants to see me direct, and I agreed. But I need players and I was hoping you might help."

"Well of course," Melia says hesitantly. "But... why would Killeen not direct?"

"The Prince wants to see Liv's skills," Joseph repeats on my behalf.

"It's kind of a bet," I lie easily. "He thinks I'm just a pretty face."

Melia gives me a disbelieving look. "No one thinks you're just a pretty face, Liv."

I give her a look from under my brows. "Why Melia, whatever could you mean?" I ask, half playful.

She makes a rude noise. "Well, that, for one thing," she says, waving a hand at me.

"So will you help me?" I ask again, needing confirmation.

"If you need me, I'm there." Joseph is stalwart, still making up for his earlier slip and trying to set an example for Melia.

"Thank you," I say softly. "And you? Will you help me, Melia? Please?"

She flushes again - for a player, Melia doesn't cope well with too much attention. "Of course," she says in an embarrassed rush. "Whatever you need."

"Need? What could Liv possibly need?" Killeen's voice is hard. I freeze, then glance up at where he's standing leaning casually against the doorframe of his room. His eyes are red. How did I miss that he'd already returned to the suite? I'm a fool. The air suddenly feels too thick to breathe.

"Oh it's no big deal," I say, playing for all I'm worth. "Thanks for worrying though." I'm hoping he takes this flattery and ceases his questions.

"Why would I worry about you?" He sneers, stepping into the room. I sit upright, every nerve alight. Danger.

"It's really no big deal," Joseph repeats, but it's already clear it's too late. I swallow. Is it possible Killeen heard more than what he reacted to?

"These two seem to think it's no big deal," he purrs, stalking across to fill a wine glass. "Do you think it's a big deal, Melia?"

Melia's gaze flickers to mine, her fear writ large. But I can feel Killeen's eyes on me and I cannot let him see fear. Show the underbelly and it'll get cut. "It's a bet," I try, my tone light. "The Prince wants to see whether I can direct."

Killeen is a consummate performer and his sense of timing is impeccable. He is silent, trailing fingertips over the backs of arm chairs. He's getting closer to me, and I want to stand, to put myself out of his reach. But I refuse to let him see me afraid. "And why," he goes on eventually. "Would the Prince want to see the directing skills of a player? A player who already has a troupe?"

He knows. He already knows.

Fuck.

But just as I am about to rise, his big hand clamps on the back of my neck and he hoists me high, like I'm a doll. The pain sears through my neck as I hang helpless, before he tosses me across the floor to slam awkwardly into the sideboard.

"Ungrateful fucking whore."

The words hang like the sound of a slap in the air. Heat burns through my back and hip where I hit the floor. I lie still and dazed for a moment, my breath sticking in my lungs. Blood drips from my chin to the ground. I tongue at my cheek gingerly. I must've bit it as I landed but the teeth are fine. And I can't feel any pain.

A chill steals over me.

I rise, drawing myself up. Anger is like lightning, crackling through me. Joseph puts his slender form between Killeen and I, his gray eyes wide and fearful, fixed on mine.

Whatever fear I'm feeling is eons away.

"Not whore enough for you though, was I?!" I spit. "Don't fucking pretend you don't understand. Don't fucking pretend that this is me betraying you, you asshole." My face an ugly sneer. Every iota of disgust I feel for him shows, I know it, and he recoils. He really couldn't imagine I could feel like this. Gods, the entitlement. It's inconceivable. "You've made my life a long line of careful dodges of your attempts to rape me. Yes, dodging rape every day from the man who holds power over my source of fucking coin. And you're making me out to be the manipulative one here? Fucking save it."

"I have never forced anyone in my life," he says, and I can tell the barb has landed. Like most men, he prides himself on not being like those rapists. No man will ever believe himself to be bad and so whatever he does is justifiable.

"The only reason you haven't started is because I made sure you never got the chance," I snap. "Because it is crystal clear that you give not a flying fuck about what I want. Whether I want your filthy old hands pawing at my body. Your withered fucking cock in my sand-dry cunt."

His face darkens, literally, turning from red to puce. I should be afraid - should be careful - but the anger matters more right now. The searing incandescent power of finally telling him my fucking truth. He sputters, and I can't keep back the grin - almost bared teeth - at his inability to respond. "You... you fucking ungrateful fucking cunt," he bellows. "I fucking housed you. Fed you. Kept you in more coin than you've ever seen."

"And who fucking earned that coin, huh?" I yell back. "You act like I'm some stray dog you saved off the street. But are you going to try and tell me you'd have made it here, to the capital, into this fucking competition without me?" I give him another sneer. "Not fucking likely."

He lunges at me, knocking Joseph to the ground. I dodge around a chair, ignoring the stab of pain in my hip. He trips over Joseph, falling to the ground with a cry that turns into a long string of curses. Melia is sobbing, I realize abruptly, and she's edging forward carefully to try and help them both up.

I look down on Killeen, his waxed mustache askew on his face, and say derisively, "I think I'll find somewhere else to sleep tonight." I'm shaking, but its satisfying too.

"That's right, go whore yourself to the Prince," he mutters angrily, like he's not sure he can say the words. That uncertainty tells me my words have landed better than any physical attack. I swallow the lump in my throat, caution suddenly asserting itself. Too late. Joseph and Melia stare up at me from the floor, consternation writ large on their faces. They know as well as I do.

There's no coming back from this.

I draw a shaky breath. Everything now rides on the fucking Prince recognizing I can lead a troupe. When all he can see is a pretty face and a body he wants in his bed.

Fuck.

"Anyone but you," I bite off, loud and sharp, and slam the door behind me.

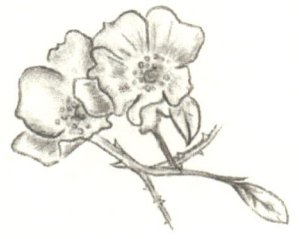

CHAPTER FOURTEEN

The hallways are quiet and still in the palace, flickering with only occasional lamplight. I make myself walk, and every step away from the suite we'd shared makes me feel both relieved and closer to tears.

I can think of only one place to hide. The Convenor has been kind, but this might stretch the friendship a little too far, even with Elouise's calling in favors for me.

But I realize abruptly as the double doors come in view that I've automatically been treading the path back to the ballroom to find them, but the thought of finding the Prince still in his cups - of having to play at stupid, or even at clever - is unbearable. I hesitate for a long moment, ducking into a shadowed niche, and the doors swing open, releasing the sounds of laughter and chatter.

It's a world away from what I've had to deal with tonight.

The cluster of people who emerge from the ballroom are gorgeously dressed, and their masks are stunning: a cockatoo, a fox, a snowy owl, a koala, a fairy wren, a quokka and a peacock with a headdress that sweeps the sides of the hallway. I can't help but smile at the sight. Their laughter is infectious. They split into two groups, kissing the air above each other's shoulders before moving in opposite directions.

The snowy owl pauses when they see me. They make some excuse to their friends, who pout and moan, one even stomping his foot, but they kiss the air over each other's shoulders, and the owl turns back toward me.

"You look like some kind of mysterious, semi-otherworldly creature, in that shadow," they say.

"Do I?" I'm aiming for nonchalant and playful but it comes out more fragile than I intended. I reach up and realize I'm still wearing the mask.

"Are you well?" They shove the owl mask back on top of their head, setting their silks whipping around their arms, and peer at me, reaching out with those long fingers to stroke my neck. "Is that a bruise?!"

The fragility makes me play even harder. I give a carefree laugh, pulling out of reach, and it sounds perfectly convincing to my ear. "It might be. I'm alright."

"Come with me," they instruct, every inch of their calm authority in their voice. They lead me swiftly through the palace, unerring in their steps. I have to skip occasionally to keep up.

And then we wind up in a dark corner, and they turn a lock in a door and we enter.

The apartment is shadowed and dark but even without light, I can make out the drape and shine of leaves. They collect a taper from the table by the door. "Stay here," they say brusquely, and duck back outside the door to the hall lamps.

The room is slowly unveiled, in rainbows of color, as they touch the flame to a series of lamps of stained glass, and wonder overtakes any of my other complicated emotions.

Their apartments are extraordinary. Plants cover the walls, hang from the ceilings and drape alongside curtains. It is as if the jungle has marched inside, unable to resist any distance from the Convenor. I smile at the incredible sight - so different from the precise grace with which they conduct themselves outside the door - and then turn to find their fingers twisting into each other.

"I don't usually bring anyone here," they say eventually, in explanation.

"I am honored." I'm too grateful that they've saved me from having to either navigate the Prince in order to find somewhere to sleep, or curl up awkwardly in some hard nook somewhere.

They hesitate a moment as if they're going to respond to this, then they frown, crossing the room to examine my neck again. "It wasn't the Prince?" they ask, as if they'd rather they didn't have to.

"No. My troupe leader," I say bluntly. "Killeen."

"He hit you?"

"He picked me up and threw me across the room," I say precisely. There's no emotion in anything I'm saying, but they're looking upset enough for the two of us.

"I... should we speak to the guard?"

I laugh, and there's an edge to it that feels like it gives me away, but I'm too tired to worry about it. "No. They won't be able to do anything. Or nothing helpful anyway."

"They can lock him up," they reply, almost indignant.

"And then he'll just blame me for making him look bad in front of the King. It'll become the reason we lose - that he loses - and then he'll just... no. Thank you."

"If you're sure..."

"I am." I step away from them. Too much closeness feels strange. "Do you have any fruit? Or water?" I'm not really hungry or thirsty but I need their eyes less focused on me.

They gaze at me a long moment, as if weighing something up. "I didn't understand all of why Elouise wanted me to help you," they say slowly. "But I get it now. Whatever you need."

Inside, I rebuff the offer, refusing to be moved by it. If there's pity sitting behind it I want none of it. "Thank you. Just water for now."

"Of course."

"And then... well, then I only need your help with blowing the mind of a man so fixated on fucking me he might not be able to even see my skills." I'm aiming for self-mocking, but I fear the desolation round the edges is audible.

The Convenor gives me a level look. "It's the King's call, is it not?"

I sigh. "He says he's too busy so he's handed over the decision to Prince Shandor."

The Convenor hands me a glass, their nose wrinkling. "That is unfortunate," they agree. "But I can put all the resources of the Royal Theatrical Troupe at your disposal for this purpose. It'll take calling in some favors, but it'll be worth it."

The relief is profound, being able to share this with someone who understand what's at stake. "But tomorrow," I say.

"Tomorrow is soon enough," they reply. "And you must be tired."

I find myself blinking back tears at even this gentle solicitude.

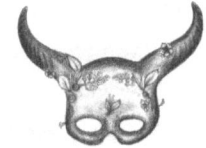

The next morning, I wake beside the Convenor, wearing one of their too-big silk shirts. I gaze at them as they sleep. They still have kohl around their eyes, despite cleaning most of their cosmetics off last night. Yet somehow they look so serene in the filtered morning light that it reminds me of joy.

I shift, and their eyes flick open, immediately alert. "Sorry," I murmur. "I didn't mean to wake you."

"It's alright," they say, stretching luxuriantly. "I'm not used to company, that's all." I glance down at their bare, narrow chest and my fingers follow my gaze, gently tracing the swirls of sparse chest hair, the tidy button of their areola. Their breath catches and they settle a hand over mine. "I… if you will go on being unbearably gentle, I have to tell you that that is the surest path to desire for me."

I grin. "I know you like gentle touch. But I thought you liked walking around carrying desire unfulfilled in your body?"

They roll their eyes at me. "Climax still wins," they say with heavy irony. "But I'm just... if all you mean by it is affection, that is as well, but I will..." they gesture awkwardly.

I shrug. "I like a bit of distraction in the morning."

"Do you now? And what if I wanted to do more than distract you?" They shift their weight towards me so that I fall back against the pillow.

"Well, I wouldn't be opposed." Desire begins its low hum in my bones. Sex is the best way for me to find my way back to myself, often. And though I hate to think on it, I always feel shaken when I fail to keep myself safe - like I've been dislodged from myself.

"Would you let me taste you?" They move above me. "Because I can think of no better start to the day."

"I would like to start your day off on a good note." I grin.

They kiss me then, and my smile fades as their mouth on mine heats my blood. I slide my fingers into their satiny black hair, and then smooth down to the nape of their neck. My touch makes them shiver and gasp and pull from the kiss. I stroke across their shoulder, curling my fingertips to trace a swirl across their chest. They gasp again, then shake their head at me. "You're very distracting. I was meant to be tasting you."

"Am I stopping you?" I ask, laughingly. "I wasn't aware."

They make a noise of grunting irritation, and then capture my nipple between their lips. I gasp, just lightly, and then as they draw it into their mouth, I moan low in the back of my throat, letting my head drop back against the pillow. "I am determined, now," they tell me in a low voice. I trace my fingertips across their back. "And no distractions."

"But you feel like satin," I whisper back. "So smooth."

"You're a terrible tease," they murmur, sliding down my body. They kiss a tender patter down my front, then graze teeth across my hip, making me gasp and slide my fingers into their hair. They gently taunt me by kissing the outline of the soft triangle between my legs, then again press an open mouth to my other hip bone, the draw of teeth across the sensitive skin like a promise of what's to come.

"You call *me* a tease," I say, panting. "Who exactly is -?"

And in answer to my question, they press their mouth to my sex, drawing their tongue firmly up against my clit. I gasp, my body bowing around the touch, my hands clutching into the silken dark hair across the back of their head, pressing them to me.

Pleasure resonates out from where their mouth is pressed hard against my clit. The heat rises through my body until I'm gaping, my hands tangling in the bedsheets, hips jerking under their weight, struggling to stay still enough to not shake them free.

"One? Or two?" They hold up fingers, and it makes me shiver to think if it.

"Two," I murmur and just as they had in the baths, they slide them inside, immediately crooking to stroke within.

It barely takes a moment.

My legs shake, and I groan then cry aloud as the orgasm sweeps through me, my back arched against the bed. I pant as the slow lassitude of the aftermath creeps into my bones. They crawl up the bed beside me, and gently catch a sweaty curl back from my cheek. "Just when I thought you couldn't get any sexier," they grin, and I laugh, a throaty chuckle.

"I owe you now," I murmur, turning into their warmth, pressing my hands against their slender chest.

"No, you don't," they say, too evenly.

I lean back, peering up at them. Are they mad? "You don't want to come?" I raise a brow. "Are you sure? You seem..." I gesture between their legs.

"I want nothing you don't want to give me," they say, with that precision that tells me there's some hurt behind this.

"I don't...," I pause, staring at their dark eyes which are carefully avoiding meeting mine. I lick my lips, and suddenly want to see them undone, this ache at the heart of them overwhelmed. "And if I want to see you lose your mind again?" I whisper, then lick salt along the length of their neck. "If I want to learn what will make you shiver and shake and give yourself over to pleasure?"

They meet my gaze finally, dark eyes solemn. I resist the urge to tease them. "Shall I tell you?" they ask, as if testing whether I'm serious.

"Tell me," I say, so deliberately seductive it's a self-deprecating pretence, and they give me a lopsided grin.

"Start as you did before. The gentle touch."

I trail fingertips up their arm, across their chest, swirling around the shoulder, then tracing a snaking line back across their ribs. They gape, and gasp, and for a moment I wonder if they're playing, but they give me a beatific smile and I realize that no, they are sincere. This tender touch is enough. Their nethers are stiff and aching. "May I?" I murmur, glancing at their face. This is so different from the first time. I can feel the vulnerability this delicate touch makes of their body.

"Yes," they say. I can hear the hesitation in their voice, so I watch them closely as I wrap my hand around their hard nethers. They twitch unhappily and I narrow my eyes, loosening my grip. Instead I slide my fingertips across the velvety skin and they shudder and moan in pleasure and relief both.

I smile. There's nothing like finding the path to another's pleasure. It feels like winning, every time. "And may I taste you?"

Again that uncertain gaze, and I can almost feel them gathering their courage. "Yes, but..."

"I think I understand," I murmur. "But you tell me if it's not right."

They give a choking laugh, and I slide down their body. I use the same trailing gentle touch across their thighs and hips, and then tease across the soft skin of their hard nethers. They shiver and moan and I grin at the sight of their nethers twitching toward me as if seeking out my mouth. I trail just the tip of my tongue up the length of it, then around the edge of the tip.

I'd been told once by Umina, a player in Picton's troupe, about a sweet spot much like a clit on a cock, at least for some. I've never encountered it before, but then I've rarely met, let alone fucked those who find their way between the space of men and women.

But when I press my lips tight against the soft, tight folds tucked into the arrowhead just below the head of their nethers, the Convenor cries out, their hands compulsively caressing my hair, as if they want to hold me in place but don't want me to feel trapped. "That," they say, gasping, after a moment. "Do that."

I grin, triumph soaring through me, and stroke my tongue over and over against this point, finding the rhythm they respond to by instinct. They moan, breath catching in their throat. I reach forward, sliding gentle hands up and across their chest, around the areolae, plucking at the nipples, and they gasp, limbs shivering. I press my tongue deep into this bundle of nerves, then give two quick light strokes before pressing into them again.

And with a sweet sharp cry, they jerk off the bed, eyes wide and unseeing, hands tightened in my hair and their nethers spilling forth cream across their stomach.

I keep my mouth pinned to the sensitive spot until they shudder and still, and then I smile up at them.

It takes a time for them to come back down enough to meet my gaze. They give a soft chuckle. "You look ridiculously pleased with yourself."

"I am," I reply comfortably. "Should I not be?"

They give another airy laugh. "No, I suppose that's fair," they murmur softly. "You... have an affinity for more than just playing, it would seem." They smile, sliding a hand through my curls, just gazing at me a long moment. "But could you find me a towel?"

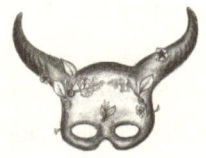

The afterglow is heady and warm, and somehow the day seems much brighter for having come beneath their gentle ministrations. They have none of the authority of Elouise or the playfulness of Des, but they know their way around desire and it leaves me with a round satisfaction.

Those long fingers were all they promised.

"So the first step," I say, as we eat pastries together on the sunny step overlooking the gardens outside their door, "is to talk my troupe-mates into joining me. Joseph and Stemen will, for sure. And Pearlene. I'm not sure about Melia and Delina. I suspect Melia is terrified after last night. They'd have to hide it from Killeen, and I'm not sure how they'd do that.... And Delina is not my biggest fan..."

"Perhaps it's less the players you need to choose first and more the play? After all, you don't know how many characters you'll need until you've chosen one, right?"

"True." I flake a croissant away in my fingers, sending crumbs flying. "Thoughts?"

"Well, he seemed to enjoy that excerpt from The Player and the Prince that you performed when you first arrived."

"Oh I hadn't thought of that! But yes. He's even taken to calling me Indella."

"Plus it will be daring, to go against his dear mama's wishes," the Convenor adds. "And he's definitely in that stage. All rebellion, no real need for it." They give me a smirk and I grin.

"That will probably work best of all, then," I reply, musing. "He's given this responsibility and he uses it to thumb his nose at his mother. Play her off his father. Plus it's an echo of he and I - like everything is really about him." I narrow my eyes. "Too obvious?"

The Convenor gives a low chuckle and shakes their head. "It's like you know how these boys work, Mistress Equitor," they tease, and I laugh. "Would you like mate? I never let anyone see me before I've had at least a cup." They rise from their step.

I grin, peering up at them. "All of these exceptions for little old me," I tease back. "But thank you, that would be most welcome."

They swat at my curls and disappear inside. I gaze about the garden, with its little fishpond half-concealed by draping willow, set alongside a wattle that has seen its way past its sunny peak. It's so restful here.

The Player and the Prince will be easy. We won't need Delina, only Melia and Pearlene. Simpler, so long as I can talk Melia past her fears. With the extraordinary array of costumes in the Theatrical Company wardrobes, we'll be well dressed. We just need a decent stage hand and someone to dress the sets. There's no way I'll be able to borrow them from Killeen.

As the Convenor re-emerges with two steaming cups, I peer up at them. "I think it's all coming together. But I need your help with a couple more things."

They smile, settling in beside me, and I wrap my fingers around the mate they hand me. Excitement is like a frisson just starting in my marrow. "I said, whatever you need. And I meant it."

CHAPTER FIFTEEN

Only a few hours later, we're equipped with a set designer, a stage hand and I've had free run of the Theatrical Troupe wardrobes to pick out costumes. The Convenor has barely left my side except to whisk costumes off to be fitted and to send messengers to the troupe's suite to summon my troupe-mates for a meeting.

We meet in what the Convenor calls the Minor Playhouse, officially known as the Eberlon Theater. I know I'm beaming as Joseph, Stemen, Pearlene and Melia hesitantly ease through the door. I can't help it. "Thanks for coming. I hope everything is alright back at the suite."

"It's probably as well you didn't come back last night," Pearlene says, and I suspect it's understatement, if the troubled looks exchanged between the others are any measure. "Killeen... well, he ought not to drink so much."

"He was furious," Melia whispers, her eyes still round with fear at the memory. "I don't... I'm not sure he'll ever forgive you."

"For performing for the Prince when he asks me? Or for not fucking him?" I ask caustically.

"I don't think either is out of his way, frankly," Joseph says in a low voice. "I think you'd be best to avoid coming back to the suite for now. He hasn't stopped drinking since you left."

"Even your messengers set him off again," Melia adds.

I swallow hard. I can't acknowledge too much of the risk I'm navigating, or there's no way any of them will follow me into this. And I need them. "I'll stay away." I shoot a glance at the Convenor and they nod once. It'll do for now. "But I need your help. Now more than ever." I draw a deep breath. "If I'm to find a path out of this troupe that isn't... violent, I need this to work."

"What is 'this'?" Stemen asks. "They said it was a bet?"

I lick my lips. "Kind of. I'm aiming to start my own troupe. But I need the King's sign off, and he's given the decision to the Prince to make."

Melia looks up, startled and with cautious joy on her face. "But isn't that a good thing? Can't you just...?" She colors a little. "I mean, wouldn't he give you whatever you asked for?"

"It would be the first time a woman had been placed in charge of a troupe. At least one acknowledged by the King." The Convenor's words are precise. "That will not happen because Liv acquiesces to sharing her bed with him." They hesitate. "In fact, her chances of success go down if he does. He needs to sincerely believe in her skill, if he's to vouch for her with his father."

Melia looks startled, as if the thought had not occurred to her.

"Alright. So... you want us?" Pearlene says. "You want us to be in your play?" Her weary eyes fix on me, and I know she can see the line I'm walking with them. I can only hope that she won't name the risk for the others. I squash the guilt ruthlessly. I haven't been able to afford guilt in years - why would this be any different?

"We're doing The Player and the Prince," I reply. "I need all of you four. Will you help me?"

There's a little chorus of "of course," but Melia doesn't join in. My weak link. She stares at her feet and I summon up my calm.

"If you really don't want to, I won't make you, Melia," I say gently. "But the performance will not be all it could be without you."

She bites her lip, her hands twisting together. "He threw you across the room," she whispers.

I firm my jaw, refusing to respond to what she's actually saying. "He did. But I am alright. Barely a bruised hip."

"I can see the bruise on your neck," she says, sounding almost broken. She's so torn. I'd almost be sympathetic but I wasn't lying earlier. Melia can play with the best of them. And her character, Ysabel, is vital to the story.

"Bruises will fade," I say. "But Melia, if I stay, you know he's going to seriously hurt me. This is my path out. Won't you help me lay it?"

I let the silence grow round. She twists her fingers together even tighter. I refuse to give her an easy out, and even when the tears slip silently down the side of her nose. "Hey, now," Stemen says to her, putting a big hand on her shoulder. "We'd never let anything happen to you, you know that, right, Melia?"

She sniffles, nodding, and then straightens her shoulders, her blue eyes meeting mine. "Alright." She swipes at her nose with her sleeve. "Alright. I'll do it."

I grip her two hands in mine. Ruthlessness. That's what it has always taken to change any of my fortunes. "Thank you," I say quietly, sincerely. That had been easier than I'd hoped. "You're going to make this play."

The rehearsal that follows is smooth, and it's somehow satisfying to set myself as the measure of whether a scene has succeeded. Where Killeen tends to lean into sensuality, I angle for the harder-hitting emotions. Where he tends to flatten out the women characters, I take joy in inviting Pearlene and Melia to deepen their characterization. I'm shifting Indella, my player character, from being a mere plaything of the men around her to a determined figure prepared to sacrifice everything to win freedom for her people.

Through it all, the Convenor, our new stage hand and the set designer all watch with a critical eye. We've completed blocking and refreshing lines for act one and two by the time the bells are chiming the late evening. Everyone looks weary, so I send them back together to the suite to eat, after extracting a promise that they'll return in the morning so we can complete the play.

"You have a talent; Elouise was right," the Convenor says. "I'm going to go and arrange you a room. But Gusa and Onidon here will no doubt have questions for you."

They are not wrong. The sun set before the two let me leave, but I walk back through the palace with my head resonating with ideas and possibilities - for set design, for timing, for lighting and sound. I'm surprised by how much this whole process ignites me up - and how I'd never been able to see it before.

I've always loved playing, and I'm good at it, but this is almost like moving from sketching with charcoal to painting with colored inks: there's so many more possible ways to shape an audience's response. I'm vibrating with choices, each one shifting the impact the story will make.

I make my way to the Convenor's suite, and when I knock, they swiftly open the door, and step back to let me enter. "How do you feel?" They ask, almost cautious.

"I feel...." I raise my hand before my eyes and find it's shaking.

"Are you alright?" They ask, more sharply. "Are you... is that fear? He can't get you here."

I shake my head, laughing. "No, it's like... have you ever seen a tuning fork?"

They give me a disbelieving look. "Oh once or twice." The sarcasm is thick in their voice.

I ignore the sass. "I feel like a struck tuning fork," I say slowly. "Like I'm coming awake. Coming to myself."

They tilt their head at me, expression sober. "Why do I get the sense you're not going to sleep tonight?"

"I doubt I'll be able to," I laugh. "Truly. I have... my thoughts are chasing each other around in my head. It's... incredible." I gather myself a little. "But thank you. I am very conscious that it is ludicrous good luck that I have you on my side in this."

They hesitate a moment, just watching me, then with half a shake of their head, say, "I owe Elouise."

I nod. "I am still grateful. For myself."

They rise and cross the room to a large sideboard where dishes are tucked amongst plants. "I requested food enough for us both. Would you like some dinner before I show you to your new suite? It's just down the hall."

I can't quite work out, through the turmoil of my mind and emotions, whether it stings that they have found me somewhere else to sleep tonight. So I smile and nod. "Food would be good. And I hope my new rooms have as lovely a garden access as yours."

They seem to hesitate again, glancing back at me, then turning back to doling out our meals. "It's the same garden, actually," they say, a little awkwardly. "I thought it might make... you seemed to enjoy it so much this morning."

I watch them as they set the plates down at the small table. They are creating distance, but also keeping me close. Something is going on here, but my head is already too busy to work it out. "I do love your garden," I say as I take my seat. "Thank you. You are very thoughtful." I grin. "A much gentler soul than I'd have imagined the first time I met you."

"Well, that is my Convenor persona," they reply archly. "It's meant to be intimidating."

The food is good - rice with murnong curry - and I swallow a giant mouthful before I say, "I just realized - I don't even know your name. I keep thinking of you as the Convenor."

"Almost everyone does," they say, and there's a note of wistfulness or grief that catches in their voice.

I take another few mouthfuls before I realize they're not going to tell me without prompting. I hesitate. Is this a boundary they don't want overstepped? Usually I don't care about such things, but they have been so gracious and generous and careful with my limits that it makes me want to return the favor. "You don't have to tell me if you don't want to," I say finally. "But you might quite like the sound of me gasping it in your ear." They look up at me, scandalized out of whatever blue moment they've been caught in, and that shock of a smile crosses their face. "Just saying." I shrug.

"That... is..." they splutter, then draw a breath. Their voice drops a notch. "A very convincing argument."

I give them a slow smile, all the promise in it.

"I am Benjen Silvion," they say, and something about how they say it makes me wonder if I'm stepping into more than I'm intending to.

I nod slowly. "Thank you."

"You're not going to use it?"

"You're not making me gasp right now."

They laugh, and I grin back at them.

Exhaustion suddenly envelops me once my belly is full, and I barely can drag myself in Benjen's wake to my new rooms. They're sumptuous, enough to wake me just a little to appreciate them. But the weariness snaps at my heels. I collapse onto the bed. Benjen gazes down at me, their expression unreadable, and my eyelids are too heavy to keep open.

They tsk, then they're unlacing my boots, tugging off my stockings. I crack an eyelid. "I've slept in my clothes before," I say drowsily. "It would be alright."

"I know."

They roll me gently to unlace my bodice at the back and then at the front but they leave me in my chemise. "Are you protecting my modesty?" I give a sleepy chuckle.

"I wouldn't dare," they murmur in low tones.

I heave myself up the bed against the pillows. "You are too good to me," I reply. And then I crack an eyelid at them and crook a finger to summon them closer.

"Yes?"

"Closer."

They bend over me, the raven's wing of their hair brushing my cheek. I tilt my head towards their ear and in a playful gasp, say, "Thank you, Benjen."

They make a noise in the back of their throat that makes me grin in triumph. "Y-you... are a frightful tease," they say in a low tone. They hesitate for a moment above me as I grin sleepily, my eyelids drowsing shut again. "And you need sleep," they say, in their Convenor's voice. "Good night."

"Good night," I say, and roll onto my side and into sleep.

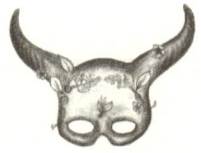

Rehearsal is smooth the next morning, and Pearlene's approving gaze on me as I explain to her what I want to shift in her performance and why, is heartening. Directing feels good.

And with every momentary success, every tiny shift that brings us closer to my ever-evolving vision, it feels more and more possible that this might actually work. Gods know I need it to: the options before me are success, abasing myself with Killeen to beg a place back in the troupe, or fleeing to Elouise, where I might lose myself forever in her arms.

"I reckon some of us might follow you, you know. If you'd have us," Pearlene tells me as we take a break, sipping at mate.

I glance at her, startled. I hadn't even let myself consider what might happen if this venture worked. It was hard enough to shove away the guilt over them risking their place with Killeen - or their physical safety, as Melia feared - to help me. I was succeeding at keeping it at bay by not thinking about the future. Ruthlessness was easier to pretend if I focussed on the right here and now. "You would?"

"You're a better director than he is," Pearlene says. "Killeen is good at picking talent, and at promoting - himself, mainly. And he's a good enough player - one of the best. It's let him gather a troupe of exceptional performers. But to be frank, it's compensated for him being pretty middling at directing." She raised a shoulder. "When was the last time any of us got any guidance on our playing from him? I reckon some might follow you because you... you have a vision, and you know how to get us there." She gives me a motherly look and pats my hand. It's unbearably moving, and I go too still. "Think about it."

I give a bark of a laugh. "I don't know if I have space in my head for that."

"That head of yours has more space than most of us would imagine." She gives me a significant look from under raised brows, and then waves her pipe at me as she makes her way outside into the garden for a smoke.

As the next few days unfold, I try not to think about what she's said. The future is far away, on the other side of this test, and there's nothing I can do about it from where we are.

But when I see the fear that occasionally appears on Melia's face at the end of a day, when she has to head back to their suite, the dream of being able to give her a place where she'd never have to be afraid is only a thought away... And when Joseph starts looking at me sadly, as if he knows a farewell is coming soon... all I want to do is reassure him there will always be space for him with me.

But I can't know that, not yet. And where I've used dreams of the future to bind others to me before - Des especially, in memories that make the self-hatred rear up like a disturbed scorpion - somehow I can't do it this time.

The sets come together more quickly than I'd have imagined, Oniden hiring on a bundle of young people to paint under his firm instruction. And the costumes reappear perfectly fitted to us, the Master of the Wardrobe giving me dark looks under his brows as I promise faithfully to take care of them.

And finally the day comes.

Benjen has been giving me space, so on the morning of the performance, I tap at their door after eating breakfast. "I have a favor to ask," I say as I step past them into their apartment.

They sigh, long-suffering, and I grin. "What more could you possibly need from me? I've put everything I can at your disposal. I'm calling in every favor I've ever had and then some."

I clasp their hands. "I need you to watch the dress," I say softly. "I need your opinion."

Their mouth falls open and I squash the desire to kiss them. This isn't the moment. They hesitate, dark eyes shuttered and I wonder if I've pushed too hard. Have I asked for too much in the midst of everything? They have been more than generous. For a moment, I'm tempted to step back and give them space, but that's not going to get it done.

I draw even closer, drawing their hands, still tangled with mine, against my chest, make my eyes round and pleading. "Please, Benjen."

They exhale in a rush and give me a sideways look that tells me both that they can see my play and that it's working. And that they resent it. I flutter my lashes and look down and they give a breathy laugh. "Blessed heavens, Liv. Enough. Leave off. I wasn't about to deny you."

I bite my lip to suppress the delighted smile, and drop their hands. "Thank you!"

"One pretty face should not have so much power," they say dryly, shaking their head at me.

"I don't know what you mean," I reply airily, dancing away across the room.

They give a loud snort. "I'm sure. When is dress?"

"Eleventh bell. We'll be done by lunch and it'll give us time to rest before the evening."

They nod. "I will come and find you."

"Promise?" I ask, my hand on the door handle and my gaze on theirs.

Their breath catches. "I promise," they say. "And you can cut that out. You've already won."

CHAPTER SIXTEEN

The Minor Playhouse is dimly lit, and the audience is hushed. This is the risky moment - a new scene slipped in between the traditional ones, devised by Pearlene and me, designed to challenge the audience's expectations and the traditional reading of this play.

My heart pounds.

I stride out onto the stage, Pearlene beside me. It was one of my careful choices, to have the head of the rebels played by a woman.

"We could not guarantee that we could make it in time," she says to me seriously. She sucks on her pipe, then busies herself at the table, inserting trailing cotton strips into clay jars. "We might not be able to keep him from killing you."

I give a sharp laugh. "I am not hoping that you will give me a safe way out. It will... you know it will work better than anything else, to galvanize the people. They know me. I'm just like they are."

She shakes her head sorrowfully. "It was only meant to be temporary. We just wanted to use your connection with the Prince to get enough food to get us through the winter. I swear it."

I shake my head. "I don't hold you responsible," I say gently. "It is not your fault. It's none of our faults. We have not dealt this hand. They have. And it's not even his fault, either. I do believe he cares for me. But this is an impossible choice for him." I jerk my head. "But you know that if he kills me, the people will know that the one Royal they were hoping might take their side... that even he will put his own place in the line for the throne above any one of our little lives."

Pearlene hesitates, clearly still torn. She scowls. "You are more than a sacrifice. We all are, but you, you especially... you have become my daughter in this long fight."

"If this will light the fuse, my life will have meant more than it could ever have meant otherwise." I grip her hands. "I will meet my death with joy, knowing it changes the world."

"You put us all to shame, commoner and nobility both," Pearlene says, her voice cracking.

"I should go, before I lose my nerve." I embrace her fiercely. "Win our freedom, Mother of All. Do not let any of our deaths, small as we are told they are, be in vain."

She grips my arm. "It has been an honor to know you," she croaks.

"And you." I pause, then raise my fist. "For freedom."

Pearlene, tears tracking down her face, raises her own fist. And the stagehands dim the lamps lighting the stage.

We move, Stemen joining me on the stage. And as we trace through the terrible steps of the final scene, playing them almost entirely as we had that first day in the Throne Room, I can feel the tension in the room rise.

When I unfurl the red silk from the hilt of the blade and collapse to the ground, the audience gasps and murmurs softly. They hush as Stemen bellows, "No! Indella, no!" I keep my body limp as he clutches me to him. He bows his head and then raises it again and cries,"Why? Blessed heavens why would you take her from me?" to the ceiling. "She was all that is good in this world..."

And on that note, freighted with what I hope is new meaning for the audience, the curtains drop before us.

I scramble to my feet, Stemen gripping my arm to help me up. A stagehand holds out hands for the dagger and catches it neatly when I toss it. And as he does, the applause begins.

It starts slowly and I have a moment of panic that something has gone awry, but as the curtains draw back for us to take a final bow, I see a host of servants lighting lamps all around the playhouse. And the entire audience, small though it may be, is already on its feet.

As I watch, I see women and even men wiping at their eyes, stamping their feet like commoners in a tent. I see the Prince, his face alight, applauding and turning to his neighbors smiling and speaking. He looks proud. And I see Benjen, their face an expression I cannot interpret, clapping so hard I fear they'll injure their hands. "You did it!" They mouth at me.

He can't deny me after this, surely?

And for a moment, borne on the wave of applause, the triumph exceeds anything I've ever felt. Better even than the best sex.

"A soirée in my suite, to celebrate this extraordinary performance," the Prince bellows. "And most especially its lead, my Indella, Mistress Livinia Equitor!"

"So he does know your name," Pearlene murmurs in my ear.

And I grin, turning to face the audience again, and curtsy as deeply as I can. The Prince's gaze on my face is just as hungry as it ever was, but there's something else in it too. I can only hope.

CHAPTER SEVENTEEN

"Here you go," Benjen says, with a dramatic flurry of golden silks. Revealed behind them is the most beautiful dress I've ever had the joy of laying eyes on. Where most of the dresses in the court have giant skirts that sit against laced bodices, this is long and silky and designed to lie against the body like a sheathe on a blade.

And it is a weapon. I can see it. It's sexy, doubtless, but it's austere as well, somehow - inviting but distant, like a sculpture. Silver silk, cut diagonally across the shoulders to reveal the edges of the collarbones in front, and the shoulder blades at the back. A neckline reaches high enough to make it look almost prim, buttoning onto the neck. That coverage is belied by the fine cobwebs of silken lace that cover the back, dipping almost indecently low. Almost. And threaded through them are a long series of small buttons curving down the back like a serpent.

It's been carefully designed to make me into an artist. One who commands respect.

"Gods, Benjen..." I whisper. "Is this... you made this?"

"I have not the skill," they reply. "But I designed it. The Master of Wardrobe oversaw putting it together."

"It's..." I trail off, speechless.

"It is. Better than I could have imagined."

"I..."

"Try it on."

They have to help me unbutton the little buttons and slide into it, tugging the silk over the swell of my breasts so it lies tight-pressed against my waist. It feels like water against my skin. They button up my back, and I can tell it's been made precisely to fit me - I have enough give to be able to move and dance and sit, but not a skerrick more. And then they gesture towards the mirror.

The woman in the mirror is regal, almost. I turn, unable to believe it's me I'm staring at. I'd known a dress could transform someone, but this? I look beautiful, yes, but cool and calm and in control, except for the riotous mass of my dark curls, like a promise of sensuality. They turn away, and pick up something I can't quite make out. "Can you kneel?" they ask.

"Gods, is this the moment for such things?" I ask teasingly, but I hitch the fine fabric up so that I can lower myself to a cushion. And against my dark hair, they arrange a silver net of tiny stars. Somehow, it makes my wild hair look controlled and sets off the muted silver of the dress, I discover before the mirror again.

"You have given me more..." I trail off. I turn to look at them, suddenly feeling as if the ground has given way beneath me. "Why are you doing all this? This isn't just for Elouise, surely?"

They lick their lips and don't meet my eyes, and answer without hesitating. "You are one of those talents that deserves to be recognized," they say. "I fought for this position precisely because it lets me be close to such artistry. And so, yes, when I see a talent like yours, I have to... lift it up. If I can."

I turn back to the mirror. "I see." It's not entirely convincing, and they're still not meeting my eyes. And then to lighten the mood, I add, "So it's not just because I fucked you, right?"

Pain lances across their face, gone in a moment and I flinch inside. Fuck. I missed it. I missed the moment when this shifted for them. I have no desire - none - to hurt them. But this... an actual impossibility, for a thousand and one reasons. Not least the Princeling waiting for me to show up to the party he is throwing in my honor.

"Of course not," they say with slow dignity. "There was no transaction. You're no jade. And nor am I."

I swallow. I have been a jade, sometimes. And I refuse to see that as a bad thing. But whatever lies between us, I know it's not that, and I know it hurts them that I keep suggesting it's an exchange. "I should get to the party."

"A dab more carmine, I think, and freshen the kohl," they recommend, stepping away. "I'll send a messenger lad to show you the way. I need to go and appear, so that no one suspects that I've been stage-managing the manipulation of the heir to the throne."

My mouth falls open a little as they turn away, their dark eyes hard. I swallow again, regretting my throwaway comment, regretting... I draw a breath, toss my head, setting the jewels in my hair sparkling. No. No regrets. It may be sad that they're feeling more about me than I am about them, but I am not responsible for it.

I meet my own gaze in the mirror and hope it's true.

The messenger boy Benjen dutifully sent for me is trotting a small distance ahead of me, and so I miss the exchange between him and a maid standing outside double doors at the end of the hallway. It's dead end, so I have to assume that these doors lead into the Prince's suite. "I... you're to wait here," the boy says to me awkwardly.

"Wait?" I repeat. "Why?"

"The Prince has a gift he wants to give you," the maid says, scanning me from top to toe, and suddenly making me feel underdressed for the evening.

I narrow my eyes at her. "What kind of gift?"

"He'll be but a moment, Mistress," she says, with a tone that borders on insolence. I give a slow, unimpressed blink, and my gaze hardens. She flushes, looking away, and the boy glances between the two of us, wondering what he's missed.

A moment later, the doors open, and the chatter, music and noise of the party emerges, followed by the Prince. Ruendon closes the door behind him, but not before giving me a swift, sharp glance that sends my heart into my shoes.

"My Indella!" the Prince cries, stepping forward. I offer a curtsy. "I beg a moment of indulgence before we join the soiree. I have a gift for you."

"It is no indulgence, your highness, if there is a gift at the other end," I say playfully. Could this be the moment? Could his gift be his approval, offered to his father?

He tucks my hand into his elbow and sets off down the hallway. "You are exceptionally clever, aren't you, Indella?"

I shrug. There's a note in his voice I don't like - and most men don't really like smart women. "I've not had nearly your education, your highness. Perhaps it's just street smarts, like a cat on their last life?"

He laughs again, striding a little too swiftly for the shoes I'm wearing. "Players are such interesting people," he tells me. "You move through so many different worlds, and with such apparent ease." He moves so that his mouth is beside my ear, and his voice is thrumming and resonant. "It makes me want to try and find something that you've never seen before."

I smile up at him determinedly. "You are the very first Prince I've ever met, I assure you, your highness. You don't need to go looking for novelty for me. I was born in Pastira, but I'd never even seen the inside of the palace until a week ago."

He pauses, turning to face me a moment, like he might say something in reply. Something has happened, and I feel out of my depth suddenly. He grips my hand, not speaking, but tugs me swiftly along corridor after corridor. Courtiers greet him with gallant and graceful courtesies, and he barely acknowledges them. Except one.

"Prince Shandor. Will you not introduce me? Your companion... she is the performer, from tonight, is she not?"

Shandor hesitates, and I stare at the man who has confronted him so baldly. He's handsome, but something about him makes me feel uneasy. Maybe it's just the Prince's reaction that's setting my nerves on edge? He clearly doesn't want to stop. But he does. He gives the man a swift, precise bow - and my gut nearly drops. At that depth, this man could be a King, or at least another Prince.

"Mistress Equitor," he says briskly, unwillingly. "Allow me to introduce you to his majesty, King Tari of Ascelin."

My heart skips a beat at the sudden realization I'm meeting more royalty, but I sink into a deep curtsy. Tari rises, bowing, and reaches out to take my hand. "Mistress Equitor," he says, in an unfamiliar accent. He brushes his lips gently over the back of my hand, and I nearly snatch it back. "You were the director of the extraordinary performance tonight, were you not? As well as taking one of the lead roles - what an achievement! Rescalin is indeed lucky that you call this kingdom home. I am unsurprised that the Prince would seek to honor your talent with this delightful party."

"I - why, thank you, your majesty," I reply hesitantly, rising to meet his eyes. The hairs on the back of my neck immediately rise. The colored iris of his eyes is so pale as to match the whites of his eyes. I make myself smile, controlling my reaction. Is that all it is? His eyes? "You are too kind."

"Not at all! If it were not the kind of thing that might cause an international incident, I might offer you a place at my own court. I know many of my friends would appreciate your... skills." He scans me top to toe as he says this, and I nearly roll my eyes. Excellent. An invitation to become an international courtesan. It seems like every man in range has plans for my future - none of which align with my own.

I laugh, that same light laugh that I've perfected through long playing. "I would not be averse to a visit, your majesty! But I'm hoping to have my own troupe soon - perhaps we might plot Ascelin into our tour. Rescalese troupes often do!"

"Does that mean you've already seen Ascelin?" His gaze rests on my face, and unease slides through me. Something about this man is setting off every intuition about danger I've ever had.

I smile. "Indeed. Only a tour or two. With my previous employer. My current troupe master prefers to remain with Rescalin's bounds. He lost a player before I joined his troupe, in a town in Ascelin. He still grieves him."

"I find it difficult to believe that the Royal Family has not recognized your skill before now, Mistress Equitor!" King Tari speaks before Shandor can utter a word, but he sends a caustic glance to the Prince. He seems determined to set himself against him, and I wonder if he knows I'll be caught in the middle. Perhaps he doesn't care, if the chilly edge in his gaze tells us anything.

"Oh, I am sure there are uncut diamonds sparkling away in all manner of minor troupes across the kingdom," I reply easily, wondering whether I should lean into this moment to force Prince Shandor to publicly agree to supporting my claim with the King. "I am only one of many."

"Besides, she is in a troupe that is in good contention for the position of Royal Theatrical Troupe," Prince Shandor says swiftly. "And if her troupe wins, they'll live at the Palace and perform for the court. It's quite an honor. The highest in the realm. Our own personal Company."

Fuck. My heart sinks. It would suit him perfectly, to have me bound to the court, rather than out traveling the kingdom and building my own troupe. But surely...

"Well..." King Tari raises his brows at me, stroking his slender beard. "If you are not bound to the Royal Family, I do hope you would come and visit Aredoma, Mistress Equitor. I can promise you a very warm welcome."

It's difficult not to feel like a street sign with two dogs pissing against it at this moment, except that both the dogs come with an entire kingdom behind them. I can feel Prince Shandor's ire rising like steam from the surface of a heated bath. "Your highness!" I exclaim. "Did you not have something to show me?"

"Yes, I was going to show you something you'd never seen before," he says. "Good night, your majesty." He bows, barely deep enough, and King Tari chuckles us as he turn away.

"Good night," I murmur to the King, who bows at me, smirking. I strive not to blush as I hasten after the Prince, desperate not to let the assumptions he is making get to me. I've never been ashamed of having sex before now - I'm not going to be ashamed when they assume I am when I'm not.

I follow the Prince, hurrying until I'm breathless. "Your highness?" I call ahead to him. "Could you slow down?"

"Of course, of course, my apologies," he says, with poor grace. But he tucks my hand back into his elbow and leads me onward. We enter the rock-built section of the palace, and Prince Shandor leads me down a long, wide stair. "Where are we going, your highness?" I venture.

"I'm going to show you something you've certainly never seen before." The repetition makes my gut swirl unhappily.

"I'm hardly so battle-hardened that that is difficult, your highness," I say, trying again to lighten the mood. Why does he think I'm this worldly creature, suddenly? "I'm really just a girl from the streets of Pastira."

He scans me from head to toe. "In that dress? In my colors?" I swallow, suddenly realizing it's true. Was this Benjen? Had they deliberately chosen the Prince's colors to dress me in? "I don't think so. You don't need to play at the naif with me, Indella. Before tonight, I might have believed it, you know. That final scene tonight - when you performed it the first time, what, a week ago, you had me convinced. A naif, a loyal, good-hearted wench giving her life for her prince. But tonight, I saw the truth." He turns away from me immediately, striding on.

I blink at the back of his head in bewilderment. "It's a play, your highness." My gut sinks. All my cleverness, the fleshing out of the women... Fuck.

"It is," he says, rounding a corner. Six guards stand in the hallway, and my heartbeat ticks up into my throat. "But it helped me to see that you... you are not anywhere near as innocent as you pretend to be, are you? You know how to strike a bargain. But that's alright. I do too. And I still know how to impress you."

The hairs on my arms are rising, and alarm is coursing through me as he approaches the guards. I wonder if he knows how paranoid he sounds. They stand before a very large, thick wooden door, set with black iron straps. "I'm going in," he declares to them.

"Your highness... usually the King would..."

"I'm the heir," Prince Shandor states, as if daring them to disagree. "Everything behind this door belongs to my family. To me. So. I'm going in."

I can think of no way out of this situation, so I'm forced to wait, watching the anxious faces of the guards as he turns four stiff locks. He turns a crank, and the door shifts and swings inward.

Prince Shandor snatches a lantern from one of the guards and steps over the threshold, gesturing for me to follow him.

I do, every nerve still on high alert.

And my mouth falls open at the sight that greets my eyes.

"See?" He's satisfied with my response. "I knew you wouldn't have seen anything like this before."

He's brought me to the Royal Vault.

It's a giant cavern. Every surface gleams, throwing the light back in bright fragments. For a moment all I can do is blink at the incandescence, but when my eyes adjust, I swallow at the sight of all these riches.

There are giant wooden chests set against one wall, one of them thrown open to reveal the gold coins within. Tall shelves glimmer with gemstones and jewels, both set and unset, cut and uncut. The shelves seem to go on forever, but there are lower shelves set within them, stacked with gold statues and ingots and jewels set on wooden busts. Laid on velvet cushions across the top of the lower shelves are a long line of crowns and tiaras. Against the back wall are yet more statues.

I can barely breathe.

It feels like Isharin's biggest heist, multiplied by a thousand. All the wealth of Rescalin, gathered in one room.

But something about the proximity of all of this wealth makes the panic associated with Isharin's betrayal vibrate through me.

I force myself to draw a breath. Then another. Another.

"Incredible, isn't it?" the Prince says casually, wandering off down the aisle. "It's not everything, of course, but it's the best collection. I thought you'd like to see it."

"Unbelievable," I murmur, desperately aiming for calm. "I... I never thought I'd see anything like this."

He's delighted with this. I can see it in his face when he turns back toward me. "I want you to know that I do see you, Indella. You've done such an extraordinary job," he murmurs, swaying toward me. Into my space.

I can't breathe again. "Thank you."

"But you could've had me without all of that effort," he says softly, running his hand up my arm to my bare shoulder. "I would have asked you to stay here with me, no matter whether you could direct a play."

I smile desperately, trying to gather my wits enough to play my way through this. He thinks it was all to have him? How do I disabuse him of this idea without pricking his ego? "Oh, your highness," I say softly. "I couldn't have imagined... I truly only sought to impress you so that you would make a good report to your father. So I could have my own troupe. I didn't even imagine beyond that."

He glances sideways at me. A casual dismissal.

In that look, my dream shatters.

He was never going to give me what I want. He only ever saw what he wanted.

The voice in my head screams wordlessly, a wail of horror and grief. I'm trembling with the effort of keeping it inside.

"What? Oh... my father doesn't have time to be worrying about troupes and players. He's deep in negotiations with Ascelin. That's why the King is here. Objectionable man that he is. Besides, I'm almost certain he asked me to make the decision for him so he can test whether I will stick with our traditions, with our customs. No woman has ever led a troupe."

It's like a slap. I nearly stagger. "But... perhaps he thought..." I trail off. Grab hold of a shelf, shove the grief away. Away, away, down, down. What can I salvage from this? Gods, I'm going to be stuck with Killeen forever. He's going to kill me and I'm going to have to crawl back. He'll make me fuck him before he accepts me back in.

The wailing in my head crescendoes.

I can't afford to think like this.

What can I get out of this? What can I play? I draw myself up, take a long slow breath. "An extraordinary room, your highness. But this is your father's wealth, isn't it? Not yours, not yet." Play them off each other, perhaps?

He gives me an arch, amused look. This he knows how to deal with, and I'm sick with it. "It's mine too," he says. "Maybe not mine to dispense with as I will, but... You do deserve a souvenir for your performance tonight. A gift as a promise of things to come, were you to stay here, with me. You're a good player, but you have nothing left to prove, not really. And I could make the role of my mistress very appealing, I promise you, Indella. Let me see..."

I'm still shaking, despite my efforts, so I'm barely conscious of it when he pauses. He picks up a small stone carving and strides swiftly back to me. He holds it out, and drops it into my palm "Here we go! It'll fit in a pocket, and they'll never even miss it."

I stare down at the grey rock in my hand. It's carved - delicately, beautifully carved - to look like an egg covered in overlapping scales. Each scale is feathered across its face, almost like tiny fans. "What is it?" I make myself ask.

"A carving. All of the statues and artworks in here," he gestures to the stacks of paintings I hadn't even seen against the back wall, "are riches in themselves. This was probably made by some master sculptor. It wouldn't be in here if it wasn't worth a lot." He smiles at me, as if he knows he has me now. "A gift, just for you. On your directorial debut, right here in the Palace. I'm honored to have been your patron for this esteemed event." He gives me a bow with a flourish, as if he's the one who's been on stage. I think it's meant to be playful, but I can barely summon a smile for the screaming in my head.

I stare at the heavy little carving. "Your highness, I can't - "

This is easy ground for him. "Pish posh, of course you can! It's a gift from me to you! The first of many I'd like to give you, if you'll let me." He draws closer, the kind of close I know means he intends to kiss me.

After all, he's paid his jade now.

I draw a slow breath, steadying myself. "You are too kind," I say. I'm emptied out. "But we should make our way to the party before people start to talk."

"Let them talk!" he barks a laugh, and then slides his arm around me and murmurs, "And maybe we can give them something to talk about, hmm?"

I force myself to laugh. Where is my lightness, the ease that's always in reach? I look at him - really look at him. He's a weak man, that much is clear. He's handsome, though, and that first night, and even after the masquerade, I'd have fucked him without a thought.

But now?

It will feel like the final nail in the coffin of my dream, and I'm not sure if I can do that.

But it's clear he expects it, especially now.

So I turn up my face, my lips gently parting, while the scorpion inside me raises its tail in fury. He kisses me thoroughly in the treasure vault of Rescalin, while I grip a tiny statuette of a scaled egg and fight to keep the screaming in my head from emerging from my mouth.

CHAPTER EIGHTEEN

I'm in a haze as we walk back to his suite. Usually kisses and touch bring me back to myself, but I feel like I'm watching it happen to someone else: the servants in corners muttering behind their hands as they watch the Prince pin me against a wall, the angle of his jaw in the lantern-light as he presses his mouth to mine, the way my own hands clutch at his shoulders. I shiver, and he smiles as if he knows he's finally won.

I feel ill.

My head won't stop screaming.

The party stops when we enter his suite. The silence almost echoes as I stand, carefully if automatically posed in the doorway for a moment, allowing everyone to take in the wonder that is this dress. I can't keep myself from shivering.

Everything - everything I'd been hoping for - is gone.

"My friends," the Prince bellows, stepping away and presenting me with a flourish. "The extraordinary artiste who gave us such great joy this evening. May I present Mistress Livinia Equitor?"

The room erupts into applause. I offer a curtsy to them all, but even the sound of the clapping is muffled in my ears. The lights seem too bright. They are applauding a fraud. A nothing. If I was really such a player, I'd have found the right performance to convince the Prince to give me my way.

The Prince stands before me as I rise, looking down on me. "Or as I like to call her, my Indella," he adds with a secretive smile as he offers his arm. I feel sick.

His suites are beautifully, sumptuously appointed, but I can barely appreciate it. It's all cast in the same gray color - velvet and brocade and opulence - as my dress. There are even diamonds - are they diamonds? - dangling from lamps and casting sparkles into my eyes, like tears. I wish, stupidly, that I could just sit on one of the beautiful couches and sink away into the soft fabric. Disappear.

I squeeze the carving of the egg in my hand tight, wishing it had sharp edges to bring me back.

This is the last place I want to be, but I follow him across the room, and take up a place on the couch beside him. I don't disappear. He drapes a casual hand of conquest across my shoulders, and I blink and try to force myself to take in the room.

To quiet the riot inside me.

Finally the screaming voices find words, and I shudder with them. He would deny me my own way.

I raise my head and scan the room. Standing with Pearlene and Joseph and Stemen and Melia, is Benjen, their long graceful fingers wrapped around the slender stem of their wine glass.

And their gaze is on me.

I blink, trying to summon the wits to work out a way out. But suddenly, all five of them are standing above us. "You're keeping the star of the party all to yourself." Benjen pouts at the Prince. "You know that's against the rules. Her light must shine equally on all of us."

The Prince laughs. He knows he's won now, so he's gracious. "Well, come join us, then."

"I'm actually not feeling that well," I manage to say.

"Oh dear! You're not well?" Pearlene picks up the thread. She tsks maternally at me.

"I knew that sick stage hand was going to be your undoing," Benjen says severely. "It's only fortunate that it wasn't before the play. Don't you think, your highness?"

"I... yes, that is most fortunate," the Prince says, hesitantly, his gaze flicking between Benjen and me.

"But best we get you back to your suite and into bed, Liv," Stemen says cheerfully. "Sooner you're resting, the sooner you'll be back to full strength."

"And she'll need her strength, if Killeen's troupe wins the Royal Theatrical Troupe," Ruendon puts in from his place behind the Prince's chair, artfully reminding the Prince that this may not be the end of my presence at court. I send him a grateful look.

The Prince's face is full of consternation, but the scowl that keeps threatening can't quite make its way onto his face. "I... but it was to celebrate all of you!" he cries.

"Oh, your highness, that's so generous of you." Joseph glances at Melia. "Stemen can return once he's taken Liv back to her rooms, yes? And we will keep you company in the meantime."

"I'd be delighted to! Your highness, I hear you are quite the Royals player. Do you have a deck handy? Imagine being able to say I played Royals with the Crown Prince!" Melia sounds more flirtatious than I've ever heard her.

"It seems unwise to bet against the heir to the throne," Joseph teases light-heartedly. "But what is wisdom, at a party?" He laughs, and the Prince laughs with him, looking around as if he can't quite believe what's happening.

Stemen helps me up, then grins, and sweeps me up into his arms. Something makes my eyes prickle, but I suppress the tears as he turns towards the door. "Mistress Equitor is retiring for the evening," Benjen announces in their best Convenor voice. "But one final round of applause for her extraordinary performance tonight!"

I raise a hand to the room as it bursts into applause. For the first time, the clapping doesn't touch me - there's no affirmation in it, no joy to be found.

I rest my head against Stemen's broad chest as we step out into the hallway. Tears keep threatening, and eventually I draw a shuddering sob of a breath and can't keep them at bay anymore. I focus on the rock still clutched in my hand, small and grey.

"Oh, Liv," Stemen says awkwardly. "He wasn't... you didn't..."

"He didn't rape me," I say in a low voice. "But I..."

"I know that look," Benjen says, their voice grim. "Both the look on his face and on yours. He said no, didn't he?"

I curl my head deeper into Stemen's chest, my shoulders shaking as tears flood down my cheeks. "He didn't even... it wasn't even..." I shake my head. "All he could see in me was what he wanted. It's all he ever saw."

"I'm so sorry," Benjen's voice is low and sad.

"You are a good director," Stemen says comfortingly, if still a little awkward. "It will happen one day, Liv."

"He's right," Benjen says. "You're not going to let some stupid Prince stand in your way."

I hiccup a laugh, and then Benjen is somehow opening the door to my room. Stemen deposits me on the bed, and then surprises me by bending to brush tears from my cheeks with his broad thumbs. "I am sorry it didn't work out," he says softly. "Truly. But you will make it happen." He stands up, looking down at me. "I've never known someone as determined to have her own way as you, Liv." He shakes his head. "They won't know what hit 'em."

I offer him a watery smile, wishing I could believe he means the words he is saying - but he's a player, same as me - and he pretends to doff a hat and leaves the room. Back to the party.

Benjen doesn't speak, but their fingertips are gentle as they unbutton the long line down my back. I wriggle out of the dress, and the sensation of silk against my body seems to bring me back to myself, just a little. I draw a long breath. "It was silly to imagine it would work," I murmur. Nothing has ever come easy.

"No, it wasn't," Benjen replies. "You did everything you could."

"I should've kept him closer. Maybe then I could've helped him see that the condition for having me was..."

Benjen shakes their head. "It wouldn't have helped. Not with him. And if you'd had to give him yourself, I don't think he would have known how to let you go afterward."

I sigh, my shoulders slumping. They bring a dressing gown to wrap around my bare shoulders, and I slip the stone egg into a pocket. "Fuck," I breathe in a low, sad huff. "I really thought..."

"It's not about you," they say softly, placing a gentle hand against my back. "It isn't. It's him. You were magnificent tonight. Truly. You outstripped anything we've seen in the competition. If you had been in the competition... I'd be telling the King he'd be a fool not to appoint you."

I laugh sadly. "You're very kind."

"I almost wish I was lying," they say, and I glance sideways at them. They avoid my gaze. "You're young, and you've a lot to learn. But you have a creative intuition I've never seen the like of..."

I shake my head. "Even if that's true..."

"I know it doesn't help," they say. "It can't make up for it. But you should know."

"It's not that," I reply. "But I've fucked up with Killeen now. I risked everything. Everything. And now..." I'll be driven back to Elouise's, and the risk of losing myself in the strange submission she induces in me.

Benjen is silent for a moment. "Let's just wait and see. We don't know what the outcome of the competition will be yet - and we don't know what any of that will do for Killeen's, uh... temper."

I sigh, and wrap my arms around my legs. "I suppose..." The tears start again in my eyes and I sniffle. "Sorry. You've been so kind..."

Benjen scrubs a hand over their face in an uncharacteristic gesture. "Gods, Liv, you're killing me here. Stop apologizing."

I shoot them a quick look, and they meet my gaze this time. For a long moment, they just hold my gaze. The honesty in their face feels like it might puncture my battered heart. I hesitate, wishing for eloquence that won't come. "I can't..." I whisper.

"I'm not asking you to," they reply softly. "This is not another demand, another transaction."

I swallow. Nothing more terrifying. "I don't even know whether to hope Killeen comes around," I murmur, changing the subject before we head into riskier territory that might bare my heart even more than I've done already. I feel so exposed, flayed raw. "Maybe it would be better for me to find my own way from here."

As if in answer, there's a pounding on the door. "Liv! Livinia!" Killeen bellows behind the door. "Open this fucking door!"

My heart stutters in my chest and then races on. Panic threads my veins. I stand up, looking around for somewhere to hide. I don't know this place. I don't know how to find somewhere to hide.

Benjen leaps up, lunging to lock the door, then turning back towards me, wide-eyed. "Quick," they hiss. "Follow me!" My breath hiccups. I am frozen, unable to move, so they grab my hand with a huff and tug me out the garden door into the night. They lock the door behind us, and then we race across the grass, and around the corner to Benjen's rooms. They flip a series of rocks in the edging of the path, feeling desperately in the dark until they find the key. I shiver, staring up at the clear sky as they open the door.

"We can call the guards. But you'll be safe here," they whisper, leading me inside.

"For how long?" I ask quietly, still shaking. I'm standing in the middle of their suites, still all darkness around me. It feels like a transgression, somehow - they'd been reluctant to have me here in the first place, and they'd been so careful to ensure I had my own place... and now here I am again. I swallow hard. "I think... I think maybe my time is up. I think maybe it's best if I just... leave."

"And go where?"

Dread crawls up my throat at the thought - at the risk that it would bring my way - but my options are almost done now. "Back to Scyless?" I twist my fingers together at the thought of appearing at Elouise's doorstep, failure of a dozen kinds in my wake. "She told me if it was a choice between harm and returning to her... there was to be no choice." She couldn't have known the terror the thought filled me with. But what options did I have?

Benjen hesitates, lighting lamps with the taper from one they'd left burning. I watch them move, their grace as they circle the room. The swoop of their movements is the first thing in this bewildering night to feel even mildly grounding. I keep my eyes trained on them, clutching after composure.

Then they turn to me, eyes wide, and I know they agree. It hurts, somehow, and I can't even work out why. "Let me go and arrange things," they say softly. Get your caravan readied. Get your horse hitched in. And I'll see if I can find out what has Killeen in such a fury."

I hate the thought of being left here on my own, but there's no way that Killeen can know where I am, so I swallow the lump of tears in my throat and nod.

"Try to sleep," they say, as they sweep a woolen cloak around their shoulders. "Everything will be alright. And Elouise will know what to do."

I lie on their bed, amongst their scent, staring at the plants that wend their vines together across the ceiling. Slow tears trickle into my hairline by my ears, and my breathing calms until, impossible as it may seem, I sleep.

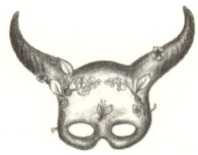

There's a gentle tap at the door and then a click. I jerk from sleep, throw myself onto the floor and roll under the bed. Just in case.

But it's Benjen, their elegant shoes dusty - likely with the sand from the courtyard by the stables. "Liv?" they ask, alarm threading their voice.

"I'm here," I say, rolling out from under the bed. "Sorry."

"You're really afraid of him," they say, horrified.

" He... he's been drinking. He wouldn't be able to keep himself from hurting me, like that."

Benjen nods once. "He yelled at the King," they say, reluctant to reinforce my fear. "About you. As if the King were poaching you from him." I close my eyes, shake my head. That stupid man. "Any chance he might have had in the competition... the King will not reward behavior like that."

I sigh, guilt coursing through me. Whatever possibilities making Royal Theatrical Troupe might have offered to Melia, Joseph, Pearlene and Stemen are gone now. And the promise of a troupe under my leadership was gone as well. My ruthlessness, stealing their futures. "Was this before or after he came to my door last night?"

"Before. I gather he blamed you for the King kicking him out."

"He kicked him out of the palace?" I ask in horror.

"Out of the celebration he crashed uninvited." Benjen's mouth twists. "But he probably will send him hence, come morning. And good riddance."

"He's only half my problem," I remind them.

"I know. I just would have hated to see him rewarded."

"But if he's leaving in the morning..."

"Your caravan is ready. Your horse hitched. And I've ordered the kitchen to stock it with food. I can send your things on separately. If you leave now, you'll be way ahead of him."

I swallow the tears that threaten. "Thank you," I say inadequately.

They give me a sad smile. "Least I could do, with this palace so full of useless men."

"I'm sure they have their uses," I say, a note of playfulness emerging in my voice. "We just haven't yet discovered them."

There's a sudden flurry, and they wrap their cloak around me, draw me against them. The tender warmth of their embrace makes tears flood my eyes. It feels like betrayal, but there's a safety in their arms, somehow. They hold me a long, long moment, then gently lift my chin. They kiss me, deeply, thoroughly enough to leave me breathless. I clutch at their shirt, staring up at them.

"I am glad to have known you, Liv Equitor. If you remember me fondly, I will be pleased."

My heart cracks a little. I wish... But I can't deal in wishes. "Always," I promise. "And I hope you know I'll be looking you up when I'm next in Pastira."

A faint smile crosses their face and I find myself smiling back, even as I know they are thinking of how complicated that would be. "I should get ready."

I dress myself in their clothes, my hips straining at the pants and the shirts flapping long around my thighs and wrists. It's almost worth it to see them laugh. I slip the little statue of the egg into my pocket. It doesn't look like much, but on the off chance it's a master sculptor's work and worth something serious, I'm not going to leave it behind for the Prince to find.

They sweep a too-long cloak around my shoulders and we hitch it up with a belt. The palace is quiet as we make our way swiftly through the hallways to the courtyard. I greet Dragon, suddenly feeling bad that I haven't come to visit him since we arrived.

"Travel safe," Benjen says in their Convenor's voice. "And give my regards to the Duchess." I realize now why they'd kissed me so thoroughly in their suites - they have to maintain their persona in front of the guards and stable hands in the courtyard. And anything we do out here will doubtless be reported - to the Prince, to the King, to the gossip-mill.

I summon up the strength to play, a final performance for the Royal court, to match theirs. "Thank you," I say. "For everything." It's vague, and inadequate, and I want to at least squeeze their hand one last time before I roll out the gates.

But they have a performance to maintain, and so do I.

So I slap the reins across Dragon's back and blink back tears as I roll out, one hand on the reins, and the other tucked in my pocket, clutching the cool stone of a carved egg. Out, through the portcullis, through the gates, and through the Capital, in search of a sanctuary that might swallow me whole.

THE END... *for now!*

Join the Journey

The best bit about embarking on this publishing thing is that I get to build a relationship with you, dear reader!

I save some of the tastiest treats for my newsletter subscribers. If you haven't yet read the tragic tale of Karina, Besta, and Des, it's worth joining to get access to *A Hired Blade* for free. It's another prequel novella to the Everlands Cycle, the pair to this one.

You'll also get bridging chapters, side stories, and other cutting-room-floor tidbits, a little of my ruminations on the state of the fantasy genre, and updates about the next release.

Plus, you get the opportunity to join my ARC, beta, and street team!

Sign up and get your copy of *A Hired Blade* now!

https://dl.bookfunnel.com/v8lgspcbf3

Enjoyed this novel? You can make a big difference!

Honest reviews are the best way for me—and you—to invite new readers to join Liv on her journey. Well, reviews, and word of mouth, of course! I'd love to have the connections and, let's be real, financial backing of one of the big publishers, but I'm a baby indie author. But I do have you! And that counts for almost everything. Please leave me a review on Amazon and/or Goodreads!

About the Author

I am JC, a queer she/they flavoured author from Ballarat. I have had the privilege of living and working all over the world before settling down with beasties both human and canine in beautiful south east Australia.

Ever since I was a child, I've been entranced by stories and storytelling.

I am vastly entertained by the unchosen heroes who can't quite believe her luck—or bad luck! By fury that fills the soul and cannot be tamed. By encounters that are funny by accident. By desire that pokes its head where it's not quite wanted.

So really, it's no surprise I'm drawn to fantasy as a reader and a writer.

If this sounds like a ride you'd like to join me on, stick around.

The best way to stay in contact right now is via my mailing list or on Instagram. But I'd also love to hear from you directly, so please don't be shy.

I live, love, play, and write on Wadawurrung land. I pay my respects to elders past and present, and in solidarity express my outrage at the ongoing horror of colonisation. Sovereignty over this land was never ceded. It always was, and always will be, Aboriginal land.

You can find JC Rycroft online at: www.jcrycroft.com

Facebook: www.facebook.com/jcrycroft
TikTok: www.tiktok.com/@jcrycroft
Instagram: www.instagram.com/jcrycroft
Threads: www.threads.net/@jcrycroft
Email: contact@jcrycroft.com
Goodreads: www.goodreads.com/author/show/24259731

ACKNOWLEDGEMENTS

As always, thanks to my family and home ground, Maria, and our wonderful kid, Ameyali. The creativity could not take up space without you both making room for it. I am grateful beyond words for the unending support and love. Thank you.

Thanks always and again to Fay Lane, ever-tolerant cover designer extraordinaire, and to Rachelle Wright, Cameron Montague Taylor, and Nay Merrill, my incredible editorial and proofing team. Generous and incisive—I mean, really, who could ask for more?!

This year has brought new authors into my circle, and they've swiftly become some of my closest friends. Thanks to Shelby, for heat-seeking missile chats, cover analysis x 1000, my very first cosplayed character (and who could ask for a better Liv?!), and endlessly kind, seriously relentless support; to Paige for helping to map the darkest corners of the bookish community so I don't have to venture there, and for hyping like no other; to Sabrina for sharing experience and insights about this author thing, for spicy brainstorms, and for constantly pushing for justice. Your love, encouragement, insight, and support has been transformative.

And thanks to Hunter, who swaggered into my life with a snarky comment and has somehow managed to joyously upend a plethora of things I'd thought were settled—perhaps the least of which is this series. Thanks especially for rerouting me to a better version of me, and for the purposes of this particular novella-that-wasn't, thank you for spotting that extra-special hidden thread within Everlands and helping me to weave it back in in a new way. This book—and the series as a whole!—is wildly different, thanks to you.

And last, but certainly not least, I want to thank all the many angry women in my life—you keep me going. Injustices are everywhere, and the fury, shared, reminds us to not accept them. Love and rage, as we keep fighting for a world more livable than the one we are currently surviving.

CONTENT NOTE

Alcohol

Anxiety

Betrayal

Blood

Death of a parent (recalled)

Manipulation

Misogyny

Profanity (including plentiful use of "fuck" and "cunt," the latter usually not as an insult)

Sex (graphic-ish; plentiful; includes fisting, oral sex, implied strap)

Sexism

Sex trafficking of a child (recalled)

Trauma/PTSD (including flashbacks)

Violence, including on-page sexual assault (not rape) and physical assault by men against women

www.ingramcontent.com/pod-product-compliance
Lightning Source LLC
Chambersburg PA
CBHW060605190726
48283CB00003B/1159

9781923055049